GOOD BEASTS BAD CREATURES

Good Beasts Bad Creatures

VERONICA KRUG

Veronica Krug

Chapter 1

This book is dedicated to

My writing group, The Seascribes

Lilia Klee

Ann LePere

Sarah Swan

Loretta Potts

And Elaine Crigler, whom we miss so very much.

Lost

An old, but well-kept farmhouse sits at the end of a long drive half a mile from the main road in Bladenboro, North Carolina. A gentle breeze brush the leaves of the live oak trees that border the woods behind it. A blast of gunfire shatters the air. The beast runs full speed out of the woods away from the sound. A crack of fire again. A bullet grazes its ear. The creature is distraught, confused. It faces the farmhouse searching for him, but he is not there. It races past an old panel truck with migrant workers riding in the back as it motors up the lane between fields of freshly planted tobacco and oats. They cry out in Spanish at the strange creature running past them. Its pitch-black fur glistens in the sunlight. The animal is at least five feet in length not including its long fluffy tail. It appears to be a panther, but its head is as large as a bear's.

Another shot of gunfire echoes through the air. The migrants duck just as a beat-up Ford F-150, gun rack in the back, passes them. The passenger has a rifle pointed out of the window. The truck speeds past a John Deer tractor in the field driven by Farmer Blaine Springer kicking up dust as it motors by. He stops in time to see a black spot disappear over the horizon followed by the truck.

He stands, gazing at the melee, "Grimalkin." He slumps back onto his seat shaking his head, "Jesus, Mary and Joseph."

*

The creature runs through fields. The pick-up truck pursuing her. Every time she stops to rest, the men approach. They shoot at her and miss. A river of fastmoving water is in front of her. She jumps in. The current is pulling her under. Every time she gets her head above water to suck in a breath of air, a bullet zings past her.

Grimalkin is miles down-river before she can get footing on solid ground. With no strength left in her, she lies on the bank and immediately falls asleep. She wakes with a start to loud screeching. No men are standing over her, instead, it is raucous grackles fighting over a bug tidbit. Deer drinking from the river nearby look up and are gone before the panther can react. The beast scans her surroundings. There are woods on one side of her and a road on the other. She runs into the woods.

Grimalkin is in Rockwell, miles from the farm. The area is completely unfamiliar to her. There are not as many woods here to hide in. She sniffs the air hoping for the undeniable scent of the farm—only to detect trees, the occasional squirrel, and...people. These people don't smell like Farmer Blaine who has his own earthy musk. They smell like flowers exploded on them.

Her mother kept her close, guiding her where to find food, water and where to hide, but she lost many of her skills since living on Blaine Springer's farm. She never had to hunt on her own.

Keeping herself low to the ground she creeps along the edge of the woods. She catches a whiff of something good...blood—an injured animal perhaps? She silently pads away from the woods toward the aroma. Starvation moves her, unaware of her exposure. Her coal black pelt can be easily seen. She approaches Rob and Melanie Millers' butcher shop. There is a van parked in front. The back doors of the vehicle are open. It is the source of the irresistible scent. Grimalkin edges to toward the van.

Fresh meat is hanging inside. The van rocks as she jumps in and grabs the beef hindquarter with her razor-sharp teeth. She drags it toward the woods.

Chapter 2

Kayla Miller Sees Something

Kayla Miller gets off of the school bus at the end of her driveway. From the corner of her eye, a large dark shadow is dragging something into the woods. She stops to get a better look but sees nothing. "Weird," she shrugs. She scampers into the house, tosses her backpack onto the counter, and opens the refrigerator door looking for a snack. She gets hungry the last hour of the day in school and now it feels like forever since the last time she ate. She finds a pack of string cheese, opens it, and runs to her bedroom in her little ranch home in the town of Rockwell, North Carolina, population a whole two thousand and one-hundred people. There are no sidewalks since there is never enough traffic to need any. They do, however, have several churches in their town-

Baptist and Lutheran mainly. Her family doesn't attend any of them. There are two Dollar General stores that sell just about anything from playing cards to patio furniture.

She changes her clothes to work in her parents' shop which is next door. Her dad, Rob, has turned their detached garage into a legit butchering business. He worked in a regular butcher shop at one time but hated the job--too many restrictions. Local ranchers told him they needed an economical way to dispose of dead and dying livestock. Zoos need fresh meat to feed their lions, tigers, and bears. So, he found a need for a shop like his, quit his job, remodeled the garage with his savings, and now performs a community service butchering ungraded meat donated or sold to him by local farmers then distributes it to the North Carolina Zoo and Tiger World. He keeps his shop in spotless condition. It would completely pass any USDA inspection if, the government agency knew about it— spotless white walls, a flood of florescent lights, a huge sleek stainless-steel table with all the accessories needed for an efficient butchering operation. There is a magnetic strip along one side to mount cutting knives. A monstrous grinder is mounted on the end of the table with a gaping mouth at the top like a baby bird waiting for its regurgitated meal. At the base of it is a slide for the meat to fall blended and pulped into a gory mass into a bucket. He receives deliveries almost every day. The grinder makes a lot of noise. The neighbors don't mind because he gives them nice cuts of meat now and then. Kayla's dad added a walk-in freezer to the back of the shop to store his meat and dry ice before processing and shipping it.

Kayla's job is getting the packing boxes out, and when they're full of meat, she tops them with dry ice, seals and labels them. Sometimes, when they're really busy, she has to touch the skinned meat that was once a horse...or a cow...or a pig. She helps her parents maneuver the sides of meat onto the cutting table. It's a gross job and it took Kayla several months to think of it as meat and not something she once could pet. It's her duty as part of the family.

She's going to be fourteen soon and she would much rather hang out with friends than pack meat in a freezing cold shop—that is, if she had any. It's her dad's fault the kids in school make fun of her. He had lost his right index finger to the knuckle in his grinder a few years ago. He sold the meat to the zoo anyway. He said the tigers don't care; meat is meat. At Kayla's twelfth birthday party he walked in with her cake in his left hand and the knuckle of his missing index finger of his right hand shoved up his nose so that it looked like his whole finger was in there.

"Man, it took a lot of boogers to make this cake."

Kayla's friends looked like they were going to puke then and there. She was so embarrassed. The party ended soon after that. They call her "Booger Eater" at school even though it was her father that did it. That name has stuck all through middle school. She's glad he's not really her father. She was adopted at birth, so she doesn't know who her real parents are. Her mother says she'll tell her some-day, but is it really important? They're the only family she's ever known. *I'm sure my real father isn't as crazy as Dad. At least I know I'll never be like him.* Kayla will go into ninth grade next fall. High school. *Hopefully the kids will be mature enough to stop calling me stupid names.* She sighs deeply and moves slowly toward the back door. *I'll be cold and Dad will tell me how dumb it is to complain and put a coat on and I'll be cold and friendless forever.* When she steps out the door toward the shop, she hears screaming over the sound of the grinder in the shop.

"It sounds like Mommy!" Kayla cries and runs toward the shop. She has called her mother, *Mommy* as long as she can remember. She continues to call her that be-cause she knows how much her adopted mother likes it.

Besides...it's a habit. *The huge dark shadow near the woods again. What is it?* Kayla pushes the door to the shop open. Her father has her mother by the hair pushing her face toward the running meat grinder.

"See anything in there? No? It's because you left the van doors open! Now there is nothing to put in here except your face!" Kayla's father yells, shoving her mother's face toward the rotating blades of the grinder.

"Dad!" Kayla cries.

He shrugs calmly, lets his wife go and steps away from her. His stocky build reminding Kayla of a

Bulldog. Except when he's making horrible jokes, his mouth turns down all the time like he's very angry about something. He keeps his brown hair short as it was in the service. Kayla never touched it, but she bets it would prick her hand like a cactus.

"I wasn't going to hurt her. I was just teaching her a lesson. Your mother just cost us seven hundred dollars. I don't know how many times I told her to shut the damn van doors. Even grown-ups must be taught a lesson." "Not Mommy," Kayla cries and hugs her mother tight.

"Who would steal a whole hindquarter of beef?" Kayla's mother, Melanie cries. "It weighed over a hundred and thirty pounds."

Her father scoffs and turns away from them. He shuts off the grinder. "Get outta here. You're both useless to me today," he waves.

Melanie leads her daughter back into the house.

"What happened?" Kayla sniffs.

"We were unloading meat. When I went back to the van a hindquarter was missing. Who would take it? No dog could have carried it away." Melanie wrings her hands and paces. "I don't know what happened? Rob has told me to keep those stupid van doors closed. I was in a hurry, Agh!" She slaps herself on the forehead. "He turned on the grinder, grabbed me by the hair and pulled my head over it."

Melanie embraces her daughter, "I was never so happy to see you. I thought I was surely going to be mauled. At the same time, I feel bad that you saw that. I don't know what gets into your father."

"I saw it," Kayla says.

"Saw what?" Melanie sniffs.

"I think I saw what took the meat. It was big and black."

"What was big and black?"

"I didn't get a good look at it, but I think it was an animal."

Melanie smiles at Kayla. "Honey, what kind of animal could drag away a hundred and thirty pounds of beef? I know you're trying to make me feel better, and I truly appreciate it. Well, if there is an animal around that big, I guess I better keep things closed up, huh?" she says stroking her daughter's hair.

"I guess. I'm glad he let you go. Maybe we should leave here and go to Uncle Mike's." Kayla's father has horrible temper tantrums, and they are getting worse. Her mother gets the brunt of his anger, and he almost seems to enjoy it. She loves her father, but at the same time she is afraid of him. It's much nicer at her mother's brother, Uncle Mike's house. "We're not going anywhere. That shop is my life. Your father never really had anyone love him before.

We're his only family, you know?"

"Where is his mother and father? He never talks about them."

"He has no idea where his father is, and his mother didn't want him. He was in and out of foster homes most of his young life. Before he met me, he had never been held tenderly or told *I love you*. Showing love and accepting love is unnatural to him. He needs us."

Kayla and her mother stand in the kitchen holding each other. Her mother's warmth against her is soothing.

She closes her eyes. She smells her mother's familiar aroma of fresh air and vanilla. She strokes her mother's velvety hair.

*

Kayla loves her Uncle Mike. He lives in Denton. She wishes he could live closer so that she and her mother can just go there when her dad has one of his fits.

Uncle Mike is kind of a nerd, but he's funny. Sometimes when he talks, he makes funny faces. She can't help but smile every time she sees him. He cooks! That surprises Kayla. Her dad says only women should cook. It goes back to history that the men are the hunters and gatherers, and the women cook and keep the cave clean. He also says that Uncle Mike should have been a girl and

Melanie a boy because she's a lot more buff than her brother. Kayla knows that's because her mother has to lift heavy cuts of meat and Uncle Mike taps on computers.

When Kayla goes to Uncle Mike's she likes to go to the park across the street from his home and run.

She runs until her legs feel like rubber. When she stands still, it's like something inside her thighs are knocking on them to come out. She breathes in the fresh air deeply and feels the heat of the sun. It's the only time she feels warm.

*

A shadow falls over her mother's tear-stained face. Rob is standing in the doorway with the Bulldog frown on his face. "Listen, I'm sorry I scared you two. Sometimes it takes a good scare to do the right thing. You don't realize how hard it is to keep this family afloat. I lay awake at night thinking about it." He bows his head and places a hand on Kayla's back. "I simply freaked out. I mean, losing that meat was like a hundred-dollar bill walking out the door. I found it out back, almost cleaned off the bone. It must have been coyotes or something. You can't turn your back on nothing."

"I think I saw it when I came home from school." Kayla releases her mother and steps away from her father's touch.

He raises his eyebrows and clenches his fists. "You did? Why didn't you say something?"

Melanie moves in between Kayla and Rob. "It was a dark shadow she saw from the corner of her eyes. She wasn't sure what it was. It could've been just a crow flying past or something."

Rob rubs the spikes of his hair with his hands and growls. Squinching his eyes closed tight; he paces. Kayla's hands cup her mouth as she cowers against her mother.

He swings his hands away as though his hair stabbed them. "Aagh!" His chest grows from deep inhale of breath. Kayla is sure one of his fits of anger is coming on.

"Follow me, you got work to do!"

Melanie moves to follow Rob. He swings around to face his daughter. "Not you...Kayla. You go make dinner. Kayla is going to clean my shop."

Kayla swallows back tears. She feels as though stuck in quick sand.

"Now!"

Freed from the pull of fear, Kayla runs to the shop, closely followed by her father.

Chapter 3

Jerry

In the town of Clayton, North Carolina, a hundred and fifty miles away...

"Where the hell is the remote?" Jerry's pa yells.

"It's...in...in the...side...table," Jerry answers.

"This place it too clean, I can't find diddly here," Pa grouches as he opens the side table drawer and pulls out the remote. He plops down on his oversized easy chair. The chair has seen much better years as it's velveteen cover has now become threadbare. The seat has a permanent indent created by his father's backside.

An old, crocheted orange and brown blanket is draped over its blemishes. He clicks mindlessly on the remote while staring hypnotically at the wide-screen television.

"Quit yer gripin', I taught the boy well. He likes cleaning this dump...doncha boy?" Jerry's mother, Maude, nods his way as she sits on her place on the sofa.

Jerry nods back and smiles meekly.

"Useless as tits on a warthog," Pa grumbles.

"What you say?" Maude yells leaning forward from her perch.

Pa only stares at the TV.

"Jerry, git your pa's medicine. It's time," she orders.

"O...kay," Jerry replies and quickly runs into the kitchen. He opens a cabinet door to reveal a cabinet full of bottles and vials of medicine.

Jerry's pediatrician identified him with Apraxia of Speech when he was three. He learned to talk much later than his peers. He received regular beatings for his inability to understand what his parents wanted from him. He wet the bed until he was ten--mainly out of fear to get up to use the bathroom and disturb his parents' sleep. By no means was he a handsome child, but he did have a face a mother could love. Now, he has a full dark head of unkempt hair, and his right eye has a bit of a droop to it. His mother says it's as lazy as his tongue. His speech is slow, with long pauses between words. He sometimes has trouble getting his mouth to form the sounds. He doesn't know why, they just come out that way despite his mother's commands to *speed it up, I ain't got all day!*

He was never enrolled in school. When his parents were asked about children, they would answer that their son died years ago in a home accident. Thus, Jerry sleeps in the attic and was never allowed to go outside for fear of being seen--until two years ago. Now, at age fifteen, he can step out into the fresh air, but not past the gate without permission. Their home is a fortress with an eight-foot chain-link fence surrounding it. His pa mows the grass to exactly two inches tall and he hates it when neighbor children's balls land in his yard. He calls the kids horrible names and throws the balls away. When Pa goes out running errands or mowing, Ma lets Jerry watch TV with her or listen to music. When Pa comes into the house, Jerry must wait on him or go to his room in the attic.

The medicine is for both of his parents. He can't read, so Ma marked Pa's medicine with blue dots on the labels and hers with red. He grabs all of the blue ones— five in all, and one dropper of liquid. He puts the pills in a Dixie cup and pours ginger ale into a glass. He takes the dropper and squeezes five drops of liquid into the drink. He brings it all to Pa who tosses the pills down his throat and drinks the soda down in four gulps.

While Pa takes his medicine, Jerry gazes at a framed photo sitting on the mantel of the fireplace. It's a black and white photo of his parents at a happier time. They're standing on the beach with the ocean in the background. Ma talks about the beach often. She says her time at the beach was the best of her life...until he came along.

"What ya waitin' for?" Pa yells, holding the glass at Jerry. "What a retard! Put it away and git the hell outta my hair."

Jerry grabs the glass and quickly obeys. He cleans the glass up and places it in its rightful spot in the cabinet. He knows it's time to go to his room. Climbing the stairs, he hears Ma talking to Pa. He stops out of eyesight and listens.

"Bill...Bill..." Maude calls, but there is no response from Pa. "Butt nugget!"

"Gol darn it, what now? Can't I just watch my show in peace?"

"We need to get away. Remember what a great time we had at the beach? We went fishing and you learned how to surf. Oh, you were so damn fun back then. We ain't gettin' any younger. Let's go!" Maude begs.

"We can't leave Jerry alone. He'll burn the damn place down."

"I told you I trained him well. He'll be fine for a few days," Maude stands and blocks Pa's view of his television.

He leans in his chair trying to see. "Get the hell outta my way!" He begins to unbuckle his belt.

She quickly moves.

"Shut up, we ain't goin' nowhere," Pa continues to watch his show.

Maude sighs deeply and settles into her place on the sofa.

Jerry tip toes up the stairs to his room.

Chapter 3

A Father is Gone

Kayla remembers her mother's screams. Her face only inches from the grinder's blades. She can't understand why her father is the way he is. *I hate when Dad gives Mommy lessons.* Kayla knows she can't say anything to him, or she may end up with a missing finger...or two.

He's been gone the past two weeks. He didn't say good-bye or anything like that. Kayla woke up one morning and he was gone. Her mother tells her he's probably starting a new life with another family. Kayla doesn't understand how he can leave the shop he worked so hard for, and how can another family make him any better? Melanie says she believes he went south like somewhere in Georgia, and she's going to keep the shop running. The zoos and the ranches count on them. She doesn't seem upset about Rob leaving at all.

Melanie says she needs Kayla's help in the shop. She'll hire someone when Kayla goes back to school. Kayla wishes her mother will hire someone soon so that she can be in the sun...not some cold butcher shop. She hopes her father forgives her for whatever she has done. She wants him to come home, yet at the same time, she wants him to stay away. *What if he comes back and punishes us for not taking care of the shop right? No telling what he'll do.*

Kayla thinks her job isn't all bad, it is fun learning how to drive the fork-lift and use the hoist. It's great until she sees the animals hanging on hooks inside the walk-in freezer with no heads and skin—just bone, muscle, and fat. She feels sick at first. Her mother convinces her the animals are an important connection to life. If they didn't do this job other animals will die. Kayla must wipe out the thought of cows and horses and think of them as just meat. It is hard work.

*

Kayla and her mother finally get a Sunday off. After working seven days a week in the shop for weeks, they are going to Uncle Mike's for Aunt Sheila's, baby shower. When he says, *how ya doin'*, the corner of his lip curls one way and he winks at the same time. Kayla laughs. It's nice he gets to work at home in a cozy house.

It's so cold in the shop, Kayla must wear a coat and gloves even though it's eighty degrees outside. She misses the sun.

Melanie says Uncle Mike and Aunt Sheila had been trying for years to get pregnant. She got pregnant when they quit trying. *Okay, I learned about sex and reproduction in school. How do you get pregnant without trying?* Kayla wonders. She remembers the last time she was at Uncle Mike's. It was last Christmas.

They didn't get to stay very long because her father had a bit too much of Christmas cheer and got into a fight with Uncle Mike.

The trip is just a little more than half an hour, but Uncle Mike and Aunt Sheila live in the sticks near the Uwharrie Forest, and Kayla's dad always drove. Her mother never had to use a GPS before. The shower is in the park across the street from their house and Melanie found it okay. Kayla's happy Uncle Mike will be at the shower since the fathers are supposed to stay for them now. He complained that he was supposed to go hang out with his friend, Mumert. It makes Kayla laugh for some reason.

Kayla is having a blast. There are cool kids at the park she can hang out with. They live near Uncle Mike and Aunt Sheila. Their names are Sarah and Nick. Nick is tall with wavy dark hair and deep brown eyes Kayla could fall into. He's a bit Goth looking, but he's not really into that kind of thing. He likes horror movies too. When he talks, he has to constantly wipe his bangs out of his dreamy eyes.

Sarah's so pretty Kayla is surprised she even talks to her. She's Kayla's age with long blonde hair that forms itself into finger curls, not the straight dishwater blonde hair Kayla has. Sarah looks prissy, but she can hang like one of the guys. She gave Nick a good bruise on his arm when he dared her to hit him. She has attitude.

"I bet you're popular in school," Kayla says to Sarah.

"I get teased a lot."

"For what?" Sarah asks.

"For anything...mostly about my Dad and our shop. They say, keep your pets away from her or she'll butcher them and feed them to the tigers in the zoo. Gah! I hate that."

"You don't do that do you?"

"What? No!" *Oh man, now she's going to make fun of me.* Air whooshes out of her lungs. She begins to walk away.

"If you don't do that, why worry about what they say? Those kids sound pretty ignorant to me," Sarah opens a bag of chips.

Kayla spins around. "I know...right?" *Someone who understands!*

"My mother makes me wear these clothes," Sarah woefully looks down at her designer jeans.

"Your clothes are awesome. I wish Mommy would get me clothes like that."

"I would love cool, funky stuff I find at thrift shops.

I want to have my own style, but it would kill my mom.

She thinks being popular in school is important...I don't."

"Heh, I'd love to trade places with you."

"She works all the time. I hardly ever see her. You get to work with your mom," Sarah's mouth is full of chips.

"Yeah, I liked it at first, but it's so gross working with dead animals. I can't eat meat anymore," Kayla sticks out her tongue in disgust.

"I'd like it," chimes Nick. "It'd be cool seein' all those gutted and skinless beasts. I bet you got hooks hanging in your walk-in freezer."

"Yeah."

"Phenomenal. It would be like the movie,

Hellraiser," Nick rubs his hands together menacingly. "Bwahahaha!"

"Oh. My Gawd, Nicky," Sarah shoves the bag at Nick, crushing several chips.

"Hellraiser?" asks Kayla.

"Yeah, best movie ever. You gotta watch it sometime," answers Nick.

"Okay, sounds..." Before Kayla can finish her sentence, Nick is running to the other side of the park toward a huge six-foot ball.

He waves to the girls. "Come on!" The girls run over to him. "It's an Earthball."

Sure enough, it's a cloth-covered ball with an illustration of the earth on it. Nick has the girls hold it steady while he tries to balance himself on it. They find the only hill in the park, roll the ball up it and let go. Nick tries to outrun it only to get run over by it instead, making Sarah and Kayla laugh hysterically. As the three play with the ball, Nick sometimes touches Kayla's hand. It gives her goosebumps even though it's summer. When he catches her falling off of the ball, she tingles everywhere.

She's shaking.

"Are you okay?" Nick asks.

"Uh...yeah, yeah." Kayla is embarrassed, but she wants to be around him all of the time.

The three roll the ball up the hill one more time and give it a hard push not realizing Aunt Sheila's grandma is walking across the field with her cane into the path of the ball. Nick, Kayla, and Sarah run after it, but it's going too fast to catch it and it rolls right over her. Aunt Sheila grandma's wig comes off as she falls, her shiny bald head glistening in the sunlight. The kids run to her with Aunt Sheila close behind. Her grandma is screaming at them, calling the kids punks and that they'll be hearing from her lawyer. Uncle Mike runs up and helps her to her feet. Aunt Sheila grabs her wig and tries to put it back on. It lies on her grandma's head like an injured gray squirrel.

Everyone tells her "sorry", but she just huffs and limps away. Aunt Sheila says her Grandma is accident prone. It's a wonder she's alive. She's bald because lightning struck her once rendering her hairless. Once the adults are out of sight, Nick, Kayla, and Sarah laugh until they all fall over. It's the most fun Kayla has ever had her whole life.

The threesome sit on the grass recovering from the whole incident. A guttural growl rumbles near Sarah.

"Dang, Nick, didn't you just eat?"

"What?" Nick is puzzled.

"I heard your stomach growling."

"That wasn't me."

Sarah looks over at Kayla. She shrugs. Her face says *it wasn't me.*

"Well, it wasn't..."

The brush in the woods behind them rustle. All of them hear a growl. They bolt back to the pavilion where the party is.

"What was that?" Kayla pants.

"I don't know, but I wasn't about to stick around to find out," Sarah bends over and leans her hands on her thighs.

"Wow," Nick gasps.

When the party is over, Kayla helps Aunt Sheila put her gifts away. Melanie and Uncle Mike clean up. Sarah and Nick leave with the ball.

I sure hope I get to see them again soon, Kayla sighs.

Aunt Sheila goes straight to bed when everyone returns to the house. Kayla turns on the TV while her mother and Uncle Mike talk. She sneaks by the door to listen.

Uncle Mike dries the dishes. "The party didn't suck the whole time, I got to see you and Kayla. Hell, the last time I saw you was

Christmas...which got ruined thanks to that asshole. It's good to see you two laughing. I'm glad he left you,"

Melanie takes a deep breath and sighs, "I know."

"I can't stand to see violence of any kind toward a woman. I wanted to kill that guy."

"I'm sorry he upset you so much. It makes me feel bad."

"It's not your fault."

"I married him. That makes it my fault. I must be following tradition. Remember how we hid from our father when we were kids? The worst episode was when I was ten years old, and I saw our father choking Mom. He drank milk that was past its "use by" date out of the half full carton. It had a bit of a cheesy taste to it. He told Mom to go get him a fresh carton of milk. She said she was busy and that he'd have to go get it himself."

"I was only five then. I think I was playing in our bedroom. I just remember hearing a lot of crashing and yelling," Uncle Mike answers.

"That's when the milk went flying. He threw the open carton at her. She ducked away from it causing it to bash against a cabinet door making a combined bang/plop sound- bang-lop-splash! White, creamy fluid sprayed over the walls, counter tops and ceiling-dripping from the surfaces and onto the floor.

"He became an enraged bull charging at our mother. In desperation she threw a plate at him. He deflected it with his arm and grabbed her by the hair dragging her through the spilt milk. I ran to our bedroom, and we hid under my bed. We heard shouting, dishes breaking, fist again flesh," Melody says breathlessly.

"They had fought before. Mom was good at hiding her bruises with make-up, but this was the worst. You told me to stay put and you would get help."

"I inched my way toward the kitchen creeping with my back against the wall when the noise suddenly stopped. I peered around the corner. Mom was on her knees in front of our father--his hands around her neck-- his knuckles white from strain. Her eyes were closed. When he let go of her, she slumped to the floor. I opened my mouth to scream but only a squeak of air escaped my lips. Our father heard it and looked up to see me standing there. I ran. I ran back to our bedroom and hid under the bed beside you. My horror turned my brain off. I didn't run for help. I was angry at myself for hiding."

"You can't blame yourself. We were only kids."

"Oh, Mike, remember when we heard a deep, sudden gasp and Mom's faint voice? We were so relieved she was alive. Suddenly, our father was much calmer. We couldn't make out every word. We heard, *Sorry...you know I love you...* Our mother coughed and sucked in deep breaths. We heard her say, *I'm sorry...I should have noticed...store...be right back.* We heard the back door open and close--the heavy footfalls of our father coming up the stairs. We stopped breathing when we saw his booted feet in the threshold of our open door-then exhaled when he turned around and plodded off to his bedroom."

"Oh yeah, I remember. I thought we were hiding from a monster," Mike grips a dish tightly.

"We were," Melanie gazes at the floor. She's holding the same dish in the soapy sink since she began talking. "I won't let it happen again." The sentence harsh, almost silent.

Kayla's hand instinctively covers her mouth. "Poor Mommy and Uncle Mike," she whispers.

"I can't tell you the countless times I worry I'll be going to your funeral like Mom. She died way too young. You know that Dad did it to her," Mike holds a soup spoon like a weapon.

"I know, the blood clot to her heart was caused by one of Dad's beatings. Mike, we left her alone to deal with him."

"We begged her to leave, Mel. You even offered to have her live with you. We did all we could."

"She was afraid...and then I had to marry Rob, a man like our father. My heart had gone to him. He never felt respect or the love of a family before he met me. The stories of the abuse he suffered chills me to the bone."

"He has no pity from me. I can only hope bad karma will catch up to that jerk. I hope whoever the feeb he ran away with kicks him to the curb, and he dies homeless. If he ever comes near you or Kayla again, he will have to answer to me."

"I'm so glad you didn't turn out like our father. You have your faults, but cruelty is not one of them," Melanie smiles.

Uncle Mike is aghast. "Faults? I have faults?" he laughs. "Mel, you really shouldn't try to run the shop by yourself."

"Kayla's helping me."

"Right. Running that equipment and handling heavy meat is an accident waiting to happen. The girl needs to be enjoying summer...being a kid."

Kayla nods vigorously.

"I know, I know. I'll think about it. You know she means the world to me."

"I do," Uncle Mike gives Melanie a gentle hug.

By the time they are done talking it's after dark. Listening to the conversation has exhausted Kayla. She tiptoes back to the couch. Drifting toward sleep, she hears Uncle Mike offer his spare bedroom to them since it's late and he's worried Melanie will get lost driving home. Her mother won't hear of it. She tells Uncle Mike *Google Maps* on her phone is very dependable.

Reluctantly, Kayla rubs the sleep from her eyes, rises from the couch and goes to her mother. She leans against the threshold to the kitchen. "Mom? Why not? We can wait and go home after breakfast tomorrow."

"No, honey, we have too much to do." She turns to Uncle Mike. "We'll be fine. We had a wonderful time. You should come and see us," Melanie smiles.

"Not if Rob is there."

"I have a feeling he won't be coming back." She dries her hands on the dishtowel. "Kayla, get my purse, please? Mike, be sure to give Sheila our love."

As Melanie drives down the lane with Kayla, Uncle Mike calls out, "At least call me when you get home safe. Okay?"

Kayla's mother beeps the car horn twice.

Chapter 4

The Big Bad Biker

Melanie drives. "Damn, it's dark out here, haven't they heard of streetlights? Kayla, how soon before we turn off?"

Kayla glares at her mother's phone, turning it one way, then another. "I...I don't know. Google isn't talking to me, and I have no idea what I'm looking at," she cries.

"Let me see that," Melanie yanks the phone from her hands. "You're right. I have no earthly idea of what I'm looking at. Shoot, I knew I should have bought a Garmin."

She pulls over into what looks like a driveway. Melanie studies the screen on her phone, taps on it, shakes it; when finally, she hears a faint voice. It's Google. She turns up the volume.

"Please make a U-turn," Google says in a pleasant female voice.

"Oh, hell no," Melanie tosses her cell phone to the back of the van.

Kayla's throat hurts from choking back tears.

"Don't worry sweetheart. Think about this as an adventure. We'll eventually find our way- we..." A loud THUMP against the van with such force it rocks.

"What the...?" Melanie twists in her seat searching for the source of the impact. "How could I hit anything? The van isn't moving."

"Mommy, I'm scared. It's that big black thing. I saw it," Kayla whimpers.

"What is it? Is it hurt?"

Kayla shakes her head and shrugs. Melanie puts her hand on the door handle to exit the van to see what happened.

"No! Mommy, please don't go out there...please!" In her mind, Kayla sees her mother lean out of the car only to get eaten by the big black thing. Then, it'll reach into the van and get her.

Melanie pats Kayla's leg. "Calm down, hon. We'll be alright. I just need to make sure we don't have a flat or something." She turns the handle and opens the van door slowly.

"Mom! Please!" Kayla shouts. She knows the creature is just behind the door.

"Shhh," her mother warns as she steps out of the vehicle. No monster attack...yet. She gazes into the woods. Melanie eases around the van and sees that her tires are fine, but there is a dent in the roof. She looks at the ground looking for maybe a tree limb that has fallen, when there is a low, guttural growl.

BAM!

Kayla's face is in the window with both hands splayed on either side of her face. "Mom!" Her voice is muffled by the solid glass pane she is yelling through. Melanie rushes around the van, gets inside and locks the doors.

"Did you see it?" Kayla is shaking uncontrollably.

Melanie shakes her head *no*, trying her best to remain calm. "It's nothing...just a tree limb fell onto the roof. The van is okay."

"Why'd you lock the doors?"

"Safety first," Melanie smiles awkwardly, starting the van, and pulling out into the night forgetting to buckle her seat belt. After a few miles, she spies an open bar out in the middle of nowhere. Over fifty motorcycles are parked in the lot.

"I'm going in to get directions."

"No, don't. I'm scared. That monster might get us," Kayla whines.

"We'll be okay, just roll up your window and lock the doors," Melanie instructs.

When her mother leaves the van, Kayla rolls up her window and slams her hand onto the locks. A big hairy man creeps out of the bar and heads in their direction.

He's tall with a scraggly beard that grew all the way down to his chest. He's thin--except for a beer gut that pokes out of his leather vest. He's wearing a black and orange bandana that's wrapped around his head with the word, "Harley Davidson" pressed against his forehead. He's smiling a wide, *I'm gonna git ya* grin.

Melanie just stands there. Kayla reaches for her mother's phone in the back to call 911. It says *no service*. Kayla has seen stuff like this in horror movies. She spies the car keys on the center console. *I'll grab em and drive the van myself to get help. Poor Mommy.*

Suddenly, her mother is hugging the Sasquatch. She lets go of him and bangs on Kayla's window. She's yelling something and she's smiling. Kayla cracks open the window to hear her.

"Kayla, let me in. everything is good," Her mother knocks on the window. The man leans over her with a big lecherous smile.

Kayla shakes her head, *no.*

"Kayla, it's Mumert, Uncle Mike's best friend."

"Mumert?" Kayla kinda remembers him. *He wasn't this ugly.* She unlocks the door.

"Yeah, girly girl, you and your momma can follow me to your house. It's a nice night fer a ride anyways." It's a creepy smile.

Melanie gets in the van. Kayla leerily watches Mumert mount his motorcycle. It's all rusty. It doesn't even look like it could run, but he starts it right up.

"Really, Kayla, relax. There is nothing to fear now.

We'll be home before you know it."

When they finally get home, Kayla is so happy she goes straight to bed without saying *goodnight* to neither her mother nor Mumert. She plops down on her bed, clothes, and all, and doesn't remember anything else until the next morning. She is starving for breakfast.

She runs into the kitchen to find a note on the counter.

K K,

Busy with deliveries. Don't need your help. Relax and eat some cereal and toast.

Love, Mommy.

PS, the van is fine. Just a dent in the roof. Weird, huh?

She glances out the window toward the shop. A truck is there. A big ape of a guy is slinging sides of beef like a pillow in a pillow fight onto the forklift her mother is driving. Kayla's too hungry to watch for long, so she pours herself some cereal.

She watches some TV and reads her mother's

"People" magazine. She sees an article where Shiloh, Angelina Jolie and Brad Pitt's kid just turned fifteen. *Dang, she looks like her dad. He's cute, but...*It's almost supper time when Melanie finally comes into the house. She is dog tired. She orders pizza and then takes a shower. Her apron and a bunch of bloody rags are lying on the floor in the laundry room, so Kayla puts them in the wash with lots of bleach. She gives the pizza guy the money her mother left on the table and eats alone.

Melanie is asleep on her bed wrapped in a bath towel.

Kayla shuffles to bed. *Some life.*

Chapter 5

Feeding Time

Melanie greets her daughter at the door after she gets off of the bus home from school. "Kayla, honey, I feel bad you have to work in the shop all day, every day, so guess what? I found a man to help me. His name is Tim. His friends call him Sledge because he can throw a sledgehammer as far as a baseball. I needed someone strong enough to move the meat around. We're going on an after-hours delivery to Tiger World. I made you some soup and a sandwich. I'll be back before your bedtime." Kayla follows her mother into the kitchen. "I can eat later. I wanna go with you, please? Dad never let me go before."

"You need to eat, and we don't have time to wait. Besides, I can't watch you while I feed the tigers. I need to see how well Sledge does. He works at Tiger World part time. The tigers know him." She opens a drawer and pulls out an apron. She shoves it into her purse, as well as a pair of rubber gloves.

Kayla grabs the sandwich sitting on a plate on the counter and takes a big bite. She talks to her mother with her mouth full. "See, I'm eating. I can help you. I'll watch Hedge while you take care of the other animals. Please? Please? Please?" She takes another big bite of sandwich.

Melanie pauses to consider Kayla's request with one hand on her hip. "Wow, I just realized you'll be fourteen soon. Where does the time go? Fine, you can come along...but do everything Sledge tells you to, safety first. Got it?"

Kayla nods enthusiastically.

"And grab an apron on your way out. I don't want any blood on your clothes."

Kayla wolfs down the rest of her sandwich and grabs an apron, her excitement threatening to burp back her dinner.

Kayla's father had always made deliveries to Tiger World at night. Lea, the owner, prefers it that way to avoid any issues with the type of fare their shop produces. She doesn't want PETA on her case about using horse meat. They don't understand that it helps life go on. It's a good thing. Lea gave her the keys and told Melanie she can feed them.

Melanie drives the van and follows Sledge in his truck. Kayla notices that he takes up most of his seat.

When he opens the gate, the place is weirdly quiet.

Sledge drives slowly up the lane to the tiger enclosure. Melanie stops and gets out of the van. While he unlocks the enclosure, Melanie unloads a box and begins walking to a different part of the zoo.

"You go with Sledge," she instructs Kayla.

"Come on, K Cup," Sledge says.

Where did he come up with K Cup? "I thought your name is Hedge," Kayla smirks.

"My FRIENDS call me Sledge. You call me Tim."

He really accented the word, *friends* at her. "Do I hafta call you Tim?" He shrugs.

"Well, my right name is Kayla--not K Cup."

"Okay, K Cup. Whatever."

"Okay, Hedge," Kayla shoots back.

Kayla and Sledge enter the enclosure. Kayla's heart beats in her neck. She can't see much. She doesn't know where the tigers are until Sledge finds a light. Directly in front of her are three tigers sleeping together in a corner. Bars separate them from the beasts. The tigers blink their eyes open and stretch just like kitty cats. Their heads so huge they could easily bite Kayla's head off and swallow it whole.

Sledge tosses a few pieces of meat into their cage. They lunge at them gulping them down in a second. One of them turns toward Kayla and roars. Her chest feeling like it does when lightning is close and makes a huge boom sound.

"Come here," Sledge waves to Kayla. He approaches the gate, pulls keys out of his pocket, unlocks the cage, and nods toward the box of meat. "Stick yer hands in there and scoop up a bunch."

Kayla sticks her hands in it. The meat feels cool, soft, and squishy. She scoops it up--her hands full of ground horse meat, cow meat and whatever meat. She sees bone and tendon mixed into it. It has a metallic iron smell of blood...not really bad. The tigers smell it. They rush to the gate and roar. The thunder of their roars almost makes Kayla wet herself.

Sledge picks up a pole and pokes at the tigers. They cower back to their corner.

"Get in," he orders.

Kayla is standing there with her hands full of meat dripping with fresh blood and he wants her to go in?

Mommy said to follow Hedge's orders. Okay. He holds the pole and the gate open while she inches her way inside. The tigers roar and paw at the air. She glances over at Sledge.

"They're just big kittens," he smiles. "Here kitty, kitty," Kayla calls to them in her sweetest *here kitty* she can muster.

One of them creeps toward her while another paces on the other side of the cage. The third one lies in the corner watching intently. The first one sniffs nearing her hands. Kayla stops breathing. She hears the huff and purr emanating from him.

"Kayla!" Melanie screams. She pushes Sledge aside, rushes into the enclosure and grabs her daughter.

Kayla drops the meat. The tigers lunge for it. One of them steps on Kayla's foot as she reaches out to touch his fur, leaving a bloody mark on his back. Melanie pulls her out so fast her arm hurts.

Sledge doubles over with laughter. "Take it easy, they're as tame as kittens."

Melanie's face is red. A vein sticks out on her forehead connecting her eyebrow to her hairline. "If you ever...ever pull a trick like this again...you will regret it,
I swear you will!"

Kayla never saw her mother so mad. The tiger's fur wasn't as soft as she thought--it was kinda rough...and her foot hurts. She's told to put her foot up on the dash of the van and wait while her mother finishes delivery.

Stupid Hedge. He got me in trouble. Her mother's anger scared her. She sits with her throbbing foot on the dash and gazes at the now dried blood on her hands. She never ate raw meat before. The tigers really like it. She licks at the blood. It really tastes gross. She almost hurls. *I've tasted my own blood from a bloody nose or something like that, but this is like ass pie.* She finds a rag in the back of the van and cleans it off best she can. Her foot is okay, just a little bruised. Those cats are heavy.

The next morning, Melanie gets a call from Lea. She tells her how grateful she is for the special delivery of meat. The nit-picky tigers just love it. She was worried the shipments would stop with Rob being gone. Melanie reassures her that she will keep her stocked with meat.

Not to worry.

"Will I ever get to go with you again?" Kayla asks.

"I don't know...we'll see," which means, *no.*

"Shoot--dumb Hedge, Sledge, Tim...whatever!" Kayla grumbles.

Chapter 6

Campfire Stories

It's Kayla's fourteenth birthday. Melanie has Sledge man the shop while she takes her daughter for a ride in the van.

As Melanie drives, she tells Kayla, "I have a surprise for you. Look in the back seat."

Kayla spins in her seat and faces three bags of luggage. "Are we going to Disney World?" She watches videos online of parents surprising their kids with a trip to Disney, but all the kids are like, younger than her.

"Do you want to go to Disney World?"

Kayla shrugs, "Sure. It'll get me out of the shop at least."

Melanie chuckles, "Well, I can't afford that, but I think you'll like this surprise even more. You're going to stay at Uncle Mike's for the summer and help Aunt

Sheila with the baby when he comes."

Kayla jumps up and down on her seat. "Oh my gawd, are you serious? This is the best gift ever! I can't wait to help out with the baby." *And I'll get to see Sarah and Nicky and I'll be warm, and Uncle Mike lets me watch scary movies.* She squeezes her mother's arm with both hands. "You're the best! I'm so glad I picked you." They both laugh. Suddenly, Kayla likes Sledge since he'll be doing her work.

When they arrive at Uncle Mike's Nick and Sarah are there too. It's the best birthday Kayla can remember. Sarah gives her a cute outfit, a Free People billowy pink white and red tie-dye top and Daisy Duke denim shorts.

"We look about the same size. My mom picked it out. We thought you were a Boho type."

Kayla hugs the clothes. "This is the coolest outfit ever."

"My mom will make sure we dress right whether we want to or not," Sarah chuckles gazing at her own

clothes shaking her head. "But I do love Bohemian style."

Kayla believes Sarah is too cool for life. Nothing seems to bug her. She's smart. She knows just about everything. She says she doesn't show it at school because the kids there don't like nerds. *Why is it cool to be stupid? Doesn't make any sense to me,* Kayla wonders.

Nick gives her two *Hellraiser* DVDs—Part I and Part II. He says there are lots more. He sneaks them to Kayla when her mother isn't looking because there's no way Melanie will let her see a movie about creatures from Hell, and blood, and guts. Scary, but...Kayla can't wait to watch them.

*

Uncle Mike decides a girl's fourteenth birthday party is no place for him. He had told his friend, Mumert, about it a few weeks ago.

Mumert told him, *Bring your ass to my place. Don't need to be all surrounded by estrogen. We'll head over to Buddy's.*

Mike hasn't been to a bar in ages. He remembers getting drunk with Mumert once and they ended up at a tattoo parlor. Mumert got a tat of Yosemite Sam with his pistols blazing while standing on a Harley Davidson motorcycle. Mike watched the guy with the tattoo gun gliding it over Mumert's arm, pushing a needle in and out of his skin like at three hundred times a second--the ink from the machine mixing in with his blood. When he saw the guy wipe a trail of blood from Mumert's arm, Mike fainted. He chuckles to himself, *no tattoos for me.*

Mike met Sheila because of Mumert. Before he met her, Mike had bad luck with a woman. He thought they were madly in love and when she left him it hurt a great deal. He figured he would die a single man. He thought he was done until he and Mumert went to Buddy's Tavern and there she was--tall, blonde, with meat on her bones-- a knock out. She was with a girlfriend and the bikers were swarming her like a custom showroom motorcycle. Mumert was putting some serious pressure on her when she grabbed Mike's arm and said she's with him. Of course, Mumert knew better, but he acted real apologetic and she asked Mike to take her home. She said she felt safe with Mike because he didn't look anything like them. There was no way he could be a biker. Mike didn't know if he should've taken that as a compliment or not. Mumert likes to say Mike is his geek friend. It's okay with Mike because he got the girl.

He looks forward to cutting loose with Mumert again. When Mike arrives at Mumert's house he's met by his girlfriend, Ginger. She's holding a suitcase.

"Is that jerk with you?" she asks. Mumert's German Shepard, "Shep", ambles toward the door.

"No, I was supposed to meet him here today and go to Buddy's," Mike answers.

"He hasn't been here for weeks. I'm sick of it. He's probably shacked up with another woman, probably Missy. You know her?" Every word out of her mouth sounding like she is going to spit.

Mike shakes his head, *no.*

"I'm outta here. He's pissed me off too many times. You take care of his mangy dog till he comes back," she nods toward Shep. The dog wags his tail.

She's gone before Mike can protest the whole deal.

He goes into the house and finds some food and water for

Shep. He isn't sure what to do next, so he gets himself a beer, sits down at Mumert's table cluttered with beer cans and cigarette buts, and clears a spot to read the paper.

He hasn't answered my texts, but he never forgets his buddy, he's probably on his way, Mike believes.

*

Kayla spins in front of a mirror admiring her new outfit. "I'm so glad Mommy's letting me stay here the rest of the summer."

Sarah lies on Kayla's bed studying a catalog. "Gawd, all the girls in here look the same...skinny, with blonde hair and pouty lips. There is no definition in their legs neither. Why do you call her Mommy?"

"What?"

Sarah props herself up on one elbow. "Why do you call your mom, Mommy?"

"Cause that's what I've always called her."

"It's lame."

"What?"

"You sound like a two-year-old. Call her Mom."

"Mom?"

"Yeah, kids'll make fun of you if they hear you call her, Mommy."

"Okay, so I guess I'll call her Mom now that I'll be in high school." Kayla steps from the mirror to sit on the bed, shoulders drooping. *I'll call her Mommy when no one else is around.*

Sarah jumps up from the bed. "Let's go outside. Nick's by the campfire."

Kayla's heart leaps at the mention of Nick. "Okay."

The girls run through the kitchen. Melanie stops them. She hands Kayla marshmallows, three chocolate bars and graham crackers. "Here, make yourselves a treat," she smiles.

"Thanks, Mommy...uh, Mom."

Melanie scrunches her eyes in confusion to Kayla's correction of her name. She turns to get plates out of the cupboard. "I'll be there in a minute."

"Can we just make'm? You don't have to come out, do you?" Kayla gazes at her mother with pleading eyes.

"Oh yeah, Mel...Grey's Anatomy is on. You promised you'd watch it with me." Aunt Sheila winks at Kayla.

The women exchange glances. Melanie tilts her head and considers her growing daughter. She smiles warmly.

"Oh, yes I did. You kids go on. I'm sure you'll be fine."

Aunt Sheila is the best! "Thanks, Mom."

"Wha...?"

Before she can give a reason for calling her *Mom*, Kayla and Sarah are out the door.

*

Kayla, Sarah, and Nick sit around the campfire making S'mores. Kayla likes her marshmallow toasted just enough to be all melty inside. When she slides it off of her stick onto the chocolate bar sitting on her graham cracker, it melts it too making a yummy gooey center inside of two sweet crispy crackers. She could eat a dozen of them, but she'll only eat a few since Nick is there. She doesn't want to look like a pig.

"You know what you do around a campfire?" Nick asks.

"Play Spin the Bottle?" Sarah answers.

Kayla's face suddenly feels hot. Nick smiles slyly and looks right at her. If she plays the game, she won't know what to do. She's never been kissed before.

"Nah, that's for later."

Whew, that was close.

"We tell scary stories. I'll start. My grandpa told me there was a monster in these parts that sucked the blood out of farmers' animals. It would crush their heads first with its big, toothy jaws. Hunters came out from all over the country to catch The Beast of Bladenboro, but it ate them instead."

"Wait a minute. Bladenboro is like a hundred miles away," Sarah crosses her arms.

"Miles meant nothing to the beast. It traveled at night when everyone was asleep. Its movements like a shadow in the moonlight."

"How long ago was this?"

"A long time ago, okay?" Nick sighs.

"I saw a big dark thing a month ago. It jumped on our van," Kayla says.

"Wow, maybe it's the Beast of Bladenboro," Sarah's voice full of sarcasm.

Nick slaps his hands on his knees, leans forward and shouts, "It can't be. It was too long ago! Let me finish. Geez!"

"Should we let him finish?" Sarah asks.

Kayla laughs, "Okay."

Nick clicks his tongue, "Anyway, one hunter who survived said he saw a little one running with it. Now, it's grown and looking for fresh blood! Not far from here there have been sightings of a black beast with strange features —like yellow hypnotic eyes, big, sharp teeth and long back legs. In fact, you can call it to answer you. You must use this," Nick hands Kayla what looks like a paper towel cardboard tube. "You put one end to your lips and howl. The tube helps the sound go further so it can hear you."

Kayla is afraid to do it, yet she doesn't want them to think she's a chicken.

Sarah nods to her, "Do it!" she dares.

Kayla takes the roll, holds it to her mouth and howls her best wolf howl. They sit quietly and listen. Sarah holds up her cell phone and points it toward the woods.

"I think I see it," she whispers. "I got it on my phone."

Kayla reaches for it. "Let me see."

"Oh, my gawd, it's hideous," panic rising in Sarah's voice. "Let me see!"

Instead, Sarah hands the phone to Nick. He looks at the phone's screen and gasps, "It's uglier than I thought.

We gotta get outta here."

"Come on guys, just let me see it."

Nick finally hands Kayla the phone. There, on the full screen, in selfie mode, is Kayla with a black ring around her mouth where she had put the paper towel tube. Nick had tapped the end of it in ash from the fire pit before handing it to her. Nick and Sarah laugh.

"Very funny," Kayla laughs. Not wanting to be outdone, she comes up with her own scary story. She leans toward

Nick and whispers, "My father left us because he's in hiding."

"From what?"

"From the police. He's a serial killer."

"Tsk, right," Sarah rolls her eyes.

"It's true. Do you know about anyone around here who just disappeared?"

Sarah and Nick think for a moment. "Yeah, the head mechanic at my Uncle's garage. He went bowling one night and never came home," Nick says.

Kayla nods. "My mother took her car to his garage and my father is very jealous. He's murdered men with his bare hands just for asking Mommy...uh, Mom about the weather--and do you know what he does with the bodies?"

Nick and Sarah shake their heads. "He takes them to his butcher shop in the middle of the night and chops them up and turns them into hamburger to feed to the tigers in the zoo." Kayla takes a deep breath for dramatic pause and murmers, "They love it."

"Oh, gross," chokes Sarah.

"What about you? What happens to guys who talk to you?" Nick shudders.

"He's very protective. You'll know him by the missing index finger of his right hand. A tiger bit it off while he was feeding it." Kayla gazes into the darkness of the woods behind Nick. "He's a very bad man. It's no use going to the police because he will track you down...in fact he may be watching us now."

Nick whips around shining his flashlight into the woods. "Serious?"

"I'm serious as Aunt Sheila's grandmother," Kayla hisses.

Sarah jumps up. "Okay, that's it. Now I won't be able to sleep because of your gross stories. Ugh! I gotta go to the bathroom." She marches toward the house.

Nick stares at Kayla for a long time.

"Seriously...are you serious? Cause, Dude- that's off the chain. I'm totally freaked."

The bug-eyes and fear on his face is hilarious.

She laughs, "No, I made it up...but don't tell Sarah. Her reaction was priceless."

"Good one," Nick chortles nervously. "Do you know where your dad is?"

"No, but he wouldn't kill anyone," Kayla says, but she isn't actually sure. He worked a lot of late nights in his shop.

"So, I won't die if I give his daughter a birthday kiss?"

Kayla just about melts right there. She's trembling. She has dreamed about running her fingers through his coal black hair. She tries acting cool.

"Oh, no," She smiles, gazing up at him. A tic develops in the corner of her mouth. She attempts a pucker.

He leans in and gives her a tender kiss on the lips. A tingle makes a lightning trip from her toes to the roof of her mouth. She's covered in one giant goose-bump.

"Happy birthday," Nick's voice is dreamy.

It's Kayla's most awesome birthday ever. While Nick walks away, she has the odd feeling of being watched. She spins around to see movement in the brush.

Yellow eyes glare at her. *It's my imagination!* Kayla runs back to the house.

Sarah spends the night. They stay up watching the scary movies from Nick. Kayla barely pays attention to them as she replays Nick's kiss in her mind over and over...until one scene where a man is trapped in a meat locker that looks very much like theirs. He has no skin on him. It looks weirdly like the animals they butcher when they have no hide.

She has a nightmare. Someone is tapping on her shoulder. She awakens to see her father. He has no skin.

His face is a skull wrapped in meat. She can't tell if he's smiling because he has no lips.

"Don't look in the freezer, girly girl. Remember, don't look in the freezer. It's bad for you," he slurs.

"Why?" Kayla answers.

"Nu, uh, uh," her father sing songs while stepping away from her, window wiping his index finger.

He disappears, leaving a bloody handprint on her sheets. She screams.

Someone is tapping on her shoulder. Kayla awakens to Sarah's face ogling her.

"You okay?"

Kayla glances around the room. There are no bloody handprints on her bed.

"Uh, yeah. I just had a bad nightmare."

"Don't tell your mom. You aren't allowed to watch those movies."

Kayla nods in agreement.

Chapter 7

Mike wakes to hot breath in his face. He's lying on Mumert's couch. Shep's muzzle is over Mike's nose and he's panting and whining at him to take him outside to pee. Mike pushes Shep away, kicks some beer cans aside and groggily heads for the door. The dog rushes past him as he opens it and relieves himself on the nearest tree. Still no sign of Mumert.

It isn't like him at all. I talked to him the morning before the shower. He invited me over that day, but I had to stay. We planned to meet last night so that I could at least have one night away before the baby comes.

He decides to head over to Buddy's and see if any of them know anything. The parking lot is full of motor-cycles. Mike feels like a dork showing up in his Ford Explorer--*the ultimate Mommy car, perfect for a growing family. Sigh.*

He walks into Buddy's Tavern, a little bar out in the middle of nowhere. They could kill Mike and bury him. No one would be the wiser. Before him is a sea of beards, leather vests and tattoos...dozens of Mumerts. He goes up to the biggest one who is playing pool. He's big as a refrigerator, but he has a nice face under his five o'clock shadow. When Mike asks him if he knows Brian Mumert the whole bar erupts into laughter.

"Hell, yeah, I know Mumert. He practically lives here," the big guy chuckles.

"Can you tell me the last time he was here?"

He eyes Mike suspiciously, "Who are you?"

"I'm his friend, Mike. I was supposed to meet him last night and he never showed."

He rubs his jaw in thought. "Geez, seems like a few weeks...wow." He stops to gaze up at the ceiling in thought. The way he's rubbing his chin in concentration the hair is going to come off. "That ain't like him t'all, lest it has to do with a chick."

"His old lady hasn't seen him." Mike says *old lady* in an attempt to be cool.

"Ho, ho. I ain't talkin' bout his ol' lady." The big guy stops rubbing his chin to slap Mike in the back.

Another guy at the pool table chimes in. "Could be Tiffany. He's really into her. She's all woman." The guys in the bar laugh.

"Do you know where she lives?"

"No, that there's a state secret, but I'm pretty sure she'll be in later. I'd bet Mumert'll be with her."

"Later?"

"Yeah, like around eight. Check back then," he smiles wide enough Mike can see he has a few back teeth missing.

Mike calls Sheila and tells her all about his Mumert mystery. She agrees that he can stay one more night. Mike checks out everything he can think of at Mumert's. He sorts through the junk on the floor for a clue. He fishes through all of Mumert's drawers...nothing. Most of his clothes are strewn about the house. Mike checks his pockets, nothing but a few loose dollar bills. Shep follows Mike throughout the house. He zeros in on a pair of slacks draped on the headboard of Mumert's bed. He frantically nuzzles into one of the pockets. *It could it be a clue.* Mike reaches into the pocket to find...a dog biscuit.

He tosses it to a happy Shep.

"Do you know anything, boy?" Mike asks Shep. He just grins a dog grin and wags his tail.

Mike returns to the bar that night and meets with the big guy. He tells Mike that his name is Skillet because he likes to cook. He makes the best ribs this side of the Mississippi. He introduces Mike to Tiffany.

Tiffany is an outstanding woman with outstanding bleached blonde hair, outstanding breasts, outstanding butt, and an outstanding gut. She is, without a doubt, all woman.

"Where is Mumert?" Mike asks.

"Hell, if I know," Tiffany answers.

"The guys thought he was with you...you know, shacking up."

She laughs heartily, "Shacking up? Now, that's funny. He took me home one night and passed right out on the sofa. Kicked him out the next mornin'. Ha!" She chuckles to herself with the memory.

"How long ago was that?"

"Shit, must have been last April or somethin' like that."

Mike is barking up the wrong tree.

"Hey, buy me a drink," she smiles, flicking her platinum blonde hair from her eyes.

After a few drinks she isn't looking half bad to Mike. *She looks pretty good with blurry eyes.*

"I will rock your world," Tiffany smiles, leaning in toward Mike.

Hmm, maybe a little fun before my freedom is exchanged for dirty diapers.

Mike's thought is broken by a slap on his back.

It's Skillet. "Where's the last place you saw him?"

"He guided my sister's way home from here a few weeks ago. She got lost after leaving my house."

"Gimme her address. I'm gonna trace his route and maybe get a clue to his whereabouts."

"You'd do that?"

"Yeah, he's my buddy too. Hate to think he could be dead in a ditch somewhere."

Mike is relieved and grateful. He doesn't have time to trace Mumert's route...but Mumert would want him to have fun on his last night of freedom.

"Want to play a game of pool?" Mike picks up a pool cue.

"You?" Skillet laughs.

"Yeah, we wanna watch the little gnat hit some balls," one of Skillet's friends laugh.

Skillet picks up a cue stick while Mike racks the balls. Mike used to play pool with Mumert at the bowling alley every weekend when they were in high school. Playing a better game of pool was even the reason Mike took Physics. Now, he's aiming at the eight ball while Skillet still has five balls left on the table. Mike nods toward the pocket he wants the ball to go into.

"Corner pocket," he states.

By now he has a large audience watching. Mike stands tall with his cue stick, bends over the table, stick at ready behind the eight ball.

"He ain't gonna make it. He's gotta git it past my five ball," Skillet chuckles.

Mike tilts the stick and punts it under the cue ball, causing it to jump over Skillet's ball, hitting the eight ball into the corner pocket.

"Shit...let's do it again. Best two outta three," Skillet says rubbing his beard.

Mike beat him again...and another player...and another player. Mike plays pool until the wee hours. When he returns to Mumert's, he is greeted by Shep happily wagging his tail. Mike, too tired to pet him, plops down on Mumert's couch and falls fast asleep.

*

Mike jerks awake to his cell phone ringing in his ears. He glances at the clock. It says nine am...or maybe six...he isn't sure. He drags himself off of the couch and takes a long shower. Shep starts barking which makes his head ring. Mike's phone is going off again. It's Sheila. *Oh crap. I should have answered it the first time.* He answers.

"It's time!" Sheila screams into the phone. "The baby's coming. Get home now!"

"Are you sure?"

"I'm getting pains every half hour."

"There's plenty of time, don't panic," he tries to assure her. Mike feels panic rise in his gut which makes him throw up.

"Get here...now," she yells and hangs up.

Mike grabs his things and runs toward the door when a realization hits him. He can't leave Shep there alone. What if Mumert never comes back? He hurries back into the kitchen, jots Mumert a quick note, grabs Shep and his stuff and heads out. Shep sits in the passenger's seat like he belongs there. Mike hopes the dog will get along with the baby...and Sheila.

Mike and Sheila make it to the hospital in plenty of time. They name the baby, Noah, after Sheila's grandfather. Kayla is a proud cousin.

*

Nick and Sarah come over to see the baby.

"He's fat, his face is red, he can't walk or talk, and he poops himself. How can that be cute?" Nick asks.

Kayla slugs him in the shoulder. *Boys.*

Aunt Sheila shows Kayla how to feed, burp him, and change his diaper. Kayla loves holding him. He likes her too. Little Noah stops crying when she picks him up. Mike and Sheila are more than happy to have Kayla staying with them. Not only is she wonderful with the baby, but she also helps Aunt Sheila with the housework. They'll miss her when she goes back to Melanie.

Shep's great with the baby too. He's extremely gentle and smart. He stays right at their heels when Mike or Kayla take him on walks.

Chapter 9

Chapter 8

Missing

Her summer almost over, Aunt Sheila lets Sarah spend the night with Kayla on her last night there. Nick can only stay till ten. They have one last night by the fire-pit toasting hot dogs and marshmallows. Nick wraps his arm around Kayla. Sarah acts like she's going to throw up. Kayla wishes she could go to school with them. She thinks they're cool. No one would make fun of her here like they do at her school.

Booger eater and her Mommy chop up dogs and ponies and feed them to tigers. Stay away from her or she'll feed you to one too, they'll tease. Kayla hates it.

Nick turns her chin toward him making her forget all about the bullies at school. Kayla's only focus is on him. Sarah has left the fire pit area.

"This is our last night," he purrs.

Oh yeah, it's a purr. One of my favorite sounds in the whole wide world. He smells good too. It's "Axe". I love that stuff. It makes any sweaty teenage boy smell like a mix of pear, driftwood, and moss...so earthy, Kayla puckers up.

Nick gives her the nicest, longest, most passionate kiss of her life—his lips, firm yet soft. He's the only boy who has kissed her so far, but boy does he set the bar high. She's dizzy.

She feels something else. Nick is putting his hand up her top to touch her breast. Kayla doesn't wear a bra...yet. It startles her. She jumps back.

"I didn't mean to scare you...I just wanna...touch you. You're so beautiful and it's our last night," he says. "We'll be seeing each other again. I mean, I'm not moving to the next planet or nothin' like that," she stammers.

Kayla looks down and realizes her arms are covering her chest. She moves them away, but then waves them around like an idiot because she doesn't know what else to do with them.

"I...um...I'm going to see what's up with Sarah," she sputters and runs back to the house.

*

"Gawd, that's all boys want to do. They just want to molest us," Sarah says when Kayla tells her about Nick. She's playing with the baby. "You let them kiss you and then they think they can do whatever they want with you. Ugh!"

"Did he ever do that to you?"

"Oh gawd, no! We grew up together. It would be like making out with my brother. Ew, no way."

"Did he try it with other girls?" Kayla is hoping she's the first.

"I don't know. I'm not his babysitter. He's had a few girlfriends. I know he doesn't have one today."

"Hmm." Kayla is a little crestfallen. "He probably does it all the time. I should have known. He's too good looking not to have girlfriends."

Just then, Kayla's mother arrives at Uncle Mike's and Aunt Sheila's. She seems flustered and out of it.

Driving at night just isn't for her. In fact, she almost hit a large animal in the road. It was so black she didn't see it until it leapt in front of her. Whatever it was, it sure was fast for its size. She came early because she has a shipment to get out and she really needs her daughter's help. Kayla asks her about Sledge. Melanie says she fired him. Kayla thinks it's no loss. She didn't like him much anyway.

Her mother is fidgety and keeps going to her van to "Check on something." She doesn't even ask to see the baby. Uncle Mike offers to help her if she's having car trouble. She insists she doesn't need his help, that it's a minor issue with the van.

Walking home, footsteps pad behind Nick. It's not the *clop, clop, clop* of shoes, but more like the sound finger-nails make tapping on concrete...*click, clack, click, clack* resonating through the night air.

He stops—the sound doesn't, in fact it quickens. Nick bolts for the safety of his home. He slams the front door and listens. He hears a loud rush-brrr sound, similar to someone shooting a bottle rocket, but it's not the fourth of July. Nick closes all the blinds and curtains. He doesn't want to see what it is, and he doesn't want it to see him.

*

Melanie wakes Kayla up at 5:30am. She's had maybe three hours of sleep. Everyone else, even baby Noah, is still asleep. Kayla writes Uncle Mike and Aunt Sheila a note. She also writes one to Sarah and Noah. It isn't any fun sneaking out like that. She doesn't even get breakfast.

Kayla and her mother ride in silence even though Kayla was gone for three weeks. Melanie is sweating and wincing like she is in pain. "Are you okay?" Kayla asks her.

"Oh...I didn't want to worry you, but I had a touch of the flu. I'll be fine. I fell behind with work."

"We can hire someone else..."

"No, we can't," she snaps. "We can manage ourselves."

"But I go back to school soon. We need help."

"We'll work evenings."

"What about homework?"

Her mother doesn't answer her. Looking at her, Kayla sees a mix of fear and sorrow in her eyes. She's pale, and she looks thinner.

Poor Mommy. I'll help her until she realizes we need to hire another guy.

"So, how are things with you and Nick?" Melanie asks, changing the subject.

"Fine...he's okay."

"Do you like him?"

"Sure."

"I mean, romantically."

"Romantically? He's just a friend, Mom." *She's really asking me that.*

"Is he trustworthy? He didn't try anything with you, I hope."

"Geez, Mom...No! I told you, we're friends." *I'm not gonna tell her about Nicky--so embarrassing.*

"You remember our talk, don't you? When you started your period?"

Oh, my gawd, Mom, you had to go there. Kayla wants to put her fingers in her ears and sing, "la, la, la," so she doesn't have to hear it anymore.

"Yes, I remember all of it." Kayla remains calm. Great acting because she wants to scream, *I know everything about sex, okay?*

She turns on the radio to change the subject.

"I just want to tell you not to fall for the first guy who compliments you. Make sure he's a good man who will treat you with respect and never force you to do anything you don't want to do."

"I know, Mom," Kayla turns up the radio to drown her mother out. She glances over, deep sadness in her mother's eyes. "Mommy?" she yells over the music.

Melanie smiles warmly and turns toward her daughter. "Yes, sweetheart?" she yells back.

"I love you!"

"I love you too!"

And they both laugh.

The news comes over the radio. Just your average stuff like politics and taxes- but then the announcement that makes Kayla fear for her life—for Nick's life.

"Several men have been reported missing from our listening area, most being from Davidson County. They are Brian Mumert of Denton, Raymond Skillern of New London, Richard Greene, and Tim Michaels of Rockwell. If you have any information of the whereabouts of these men contact 911 as soon as..."

Melanie flicks off the radio. "That's here!" Kayla screams. "That's Mumert and Hedge...and is that the Mr. Greene who runs the auto-shop you and Dad go to?" *Oh, God, my campfire story is coming true.*

Her mother nods.

"This is too scary. What do you think happened? Could it be Dad?"

"Your father?"

Kayla nods in all seriousness.

"I don't think it was your father."

"But why is it people we know, except for that Skillern guy...who is he?"

Melanie shrugs.

"I think Dad knew him."

"Not a lot of people live around here. We know just about everyone. It can't be your father."

"No, no, no. Something's going on. This is scaring me. I bet Dad didn't move to Georgia. He's killing these guys...maybe we're next." Kayla's chest begins to hurt from her racing heart.

"It's probably a bad man killing bad men. You have nothing to worry about. Maybe they all just ran off ...like your father."

"That many? Uncle Mike's been looking for Mumert. He wouldn't leave without telling him. Why do you say they were bad men? Mumert was nice. He helped us."

"They're men that's why." Melanie's jaw is locked. She glares straight ahead at the road.

"Mom, I've seen Dad kill animals. I saw him hurt you. He killed guys in Iraq. Don't you think he could kill people here too?"

She continues to drive in silence. Finally, after what seems like forever, Melanie nods.

Kayla texts Nick right away: *Are you OK? Pls, just txt me and tell me ur OK.*

Seconds later, she gets a text back from him: *Yeah, r u?* (thumbs up confused face emoji)

Kayla: *Yeah, just don't talk 2 strangers. I'll explain l8tr.* (heart emoji)

Nick sends a thumbs up and a heart emoji back. Kayla's heart runs to her toes.

"Who are you texting?" Melanie asks.

Kayla doesn't want to talk any more about Nick, so she tells her mother that she is just checking on Aunt Sheila and Noah.

"They're good. I told them to watch out for Dad."

"Hmm," is her mother's only reply.

*

Mike is watching the local news when he sees pictures of the missing men on the TV screen. He recognizes Mumert and Skillet, but he doesn't know who the other guys are. Mumert's boss reported him missing. He rarely missed a day's work and he's been gone over three weeks now. Skillet disappeared three days ago leaving a wife and kids. They found his motorcycle at Tiger World, but there was no sign of him. Another man who's missing worked at Tiger World--Tim Michaels. They suspect foul play in all of the cases. The whole thing makes Mike want to locate Mumert all the more and prays he finds him safe. It doesn't sound good.

A text from Kayla chimes in: *Uncle Mike. I think my dad is killing people. Be careful. Keep Shep near u. Will u check on Nicky now and thn 4 me? I would b so grtfl.* (prayer hands emoji three times)

Pretty serious text. Could Rob really do that and why? Mumert had escorted the girls home. Skillet was just looking for Mumert. All this has gotten "True Detective".

Mike: *Don't worry K K. Shep is right here with me. We'll keep an eye on Nick for ya.* (emoji with a detective lens over one eye)

Kayla: *Thank u, thank u! Say hi to baby Noah for me?*

Mike: *Will do, b safe.*
Kayla: *U 2 xoxo*
    *

Jerry's pa sees the news and the missing men. "Maude, get a load of this," he calls out to Ma, who is in the kitchen. Jerry is doing dishes. She limps into the living room. "Whole bunch a guys is missing," he announces.

"Too bad it isn't you," she mumbles.

"What?"

"Nothin'," she glances at the TV. "Most are from Rockwell."

"What do you think happened? Maybe it's alien abductions. I told you it would happen. Their ships go everywhere. I might be next," Pa rubs the arm of his easy chair.

"Yeah, maybe whilst you're mowin' the lawn."

Pa thinks on it a moment. "Maybe...you never know. I don't want no alien probe up my arse."

"Heavens, no," Ma rolls her eyes. "Jerry should do the mowin'."

Jerry is thrilled he'll get to go outside and work, and who knows? Maybe aliens will take him to the beach.

"I'll just take my gun with me. Knowin' Jerry, he'll cut a foot off or somethin' like that, but if I go missin', tell em it was them aliens."

"Whatever," Ma limps back into the kitchen.

Chapter 9

Bullies

When Kayla and Melanie return home, Melanie backs the van to the loading door of the shop. She usually parks on the side unless she has a shipment to unload.

"What's up?" Kayla asks.

"I have to unload a few supplies for the shop. You go in and have some breakfast. Take a nap too. I know you stayed up late last night."

"I can help. You don't feel good, Mom."

"Shush, I'm fine. I'm just glad you're home. I really missed you," Melanie gives her daughter a hug.

Convinced she'll be okay Kayla goes into the house to make herself breakfast. She looks out the kitchen window. Her mother is using the hoist to take something out of the back of the van. Kayla can't make out what it is because it's covered with a heavy tarp. Melanie then begins to clean out the van. She cleans everything spotless. A habit developed from years of living with Rob. Watching her mother clean is getting boring so Kayla takes a nap.

Melanie seems much better later in the day and makes spaghetti for dinner. Kayla's favorite meal. During dinner Kayla has a million questions about her father and the other missing men.

"What could have happened? If Dad is the murderer, how is he doing it? Is he using the butcher shop when we're gone? Why would he want to kill those guys? Is he feeding them to the tigers?"

"You have a wild imagination, sweetheart," Melanie picks up Kayla's dirty dish.

"But, what if it's true? Are we safe? He tried to kill you once, remember?"

"I really don't believe your father is a murderer. He's probably laid back and chilling somewhere with some floozy."

"I'm afraid."

"There's nothing to be afraid of. I'm here. I promise I will let nothing bad happen to you, ever.

Kayla gets up from the table and hugs her mother around the neck. "You will always be Mommy to me."

A tear runs down Melanie's cheek.

*

Melanie is already working by the time Kayla wakes the next morning. She eats some cereal and hurries to the shop. The door is locked, so she bangs on it.

"Good morning, Sweetheart," her mother lets Kayla in. "Listen, just put these address labels on the boxes and help me load them into the van. If a box is too heavy, use the forklift," Melanie instructs, giving Kayla a handful of labels.

All the boxes look the same, so Kayla decides to use the forklift on all of them. Her mother continues to clean equipment.

"What label goes with what box?" Kayla shouts over to her.

"Doesn't matter, they're all the same."

Cool...easy.

The police arrive while they are loading the last box. A man in a suit introduces himself as detective Jason Billings. He asks Melanie and Kayla if they know anything about the missing men. He has a kind face and seems nice. His voice is like Mike Rowe's from the show, "Dirty Jobs". It's a pleasant deep announcer like voice.

Melanie is telling him about Mumert guiding her home when Kayla shouts, "It's my dad!"

"What?" Detective Billings asks puzzled.

"I think my dad killed those guys for helping my mom because he's a bad man...a bad man!"

"Calm down. Now, where is your father?"

"He left us a few months ago," Melanie explains. "He ran this butcher shop, but believe me, he is no murderer," she adds.

"Is there a way we can reach him?"

"He changed his cell phone number. I really don't know where he is."

"Do you mind if we look around?"

"Sure, no problem."

Detective Billings gazes around the room. "Wow, this is a clean shop, I bet you get grade A from the Department of Health."

Melanie smiles proud, "Yes, I do," she lies. The Department of Health has never been there.

"I notice on a few of your shipping labels that you have a delivery to Tiger World. We're freezing any shipments into or out of there until we are done with our investigation."

"Oh?" Melanie asks.

"We found a few things of interest which we're checking on."

"What about the tigers? They need fed." "It shouldn't take long. They'll survive just fine."

"Poor tigers," Kayla says.

Melanie asks the detective what was found other than the motorcycle. He says its classified information. He helps her unload the boxes to Tiger World. She gives him Rob's full name, birth date, and last known address. No, he didn't just disappear she tells him, and she doesn't know his phone number. When he left, he only took a few of his belongings with him. Detective Billings thanks her for the information and hands her his card.

The detective points at Kayla. "Stay alert, kiddo. Keep an eye out, will you?"

She nods her head vigorously. "Nothin'll get past me."

"Good, we'll keep in touch." He gives her a smile and a nod returning to his car. Kayla likes him. She imagines what he must be like as a father. He would never grab his wife and threaten to kill her in front of his kids.

*

The day before school starts Lea Jankorus, the owner of Tiger World, calls Melanie and tells her she was taken in for questioning. They found a dead man on her property. She's horrified. They found a motorcycle too, but it didn't belong to the dead man. The guy had puncture marks around his head. What was even worse was that the police suspected her tigers killed the men. Then, they dug up her property and had the tigers x-rayed. *Can you believe it?* Thank goodness they didn't find anything, and Melanie can resume delivery of meat to them. The puncture marks didn't match her tigers'. The police think the guy died of a drug overdose and some other animal taste tested him. They said whatever it was, is pretty big, so be careful. The guy with the motorcycle probably ran. She bet he was the dead guy's drug dealer.

I bet my dad still has something to do with it. He made it look like an animal attack...but what if it is an animal...where is Dad? Kayla thinks.

Kayla doesn't want to go to Tiger World until her father or the animal is caught. She doesn't want her mother to go there either. Kayla's glad her mother has her conceal and carry license. Kayla wants one. She's willing to shoot if she has to. *I won't let them hurt my mom, or Uncle Mike, or Aunt Sheila, or little Noah, or Sarah, or Nicky, and even Shep. I swear...I'll do it.*

Kayla dreads going back to school. She doesn't have any friends there and she's sure they're going to make fun of her. She didn't have time to shop for new school clothes. Sarah gave Kayla some of hers. Kayla wishes she could go to her school. Sarah would have her back. She's also worried about leaving her mother alone. She looks pale and tired. She insists she's fine.

*

Kayla's mother remembers the day Rob left her.

Mike and Sheila wanted them to go to an Eagles tribute concert and dinner. Melanie wanted to go badly. They hadn't gone out in ages. She approached Rob working in the shop and asked him about it. He gave her the choice of the concert and dinner with Mike and Sheila or a nice day at an amusement park with Kayla. They couldn't do both. Melanie was surprised. Kayla had asked several times to go to the park and each time Rob said *no--*costs too much, too hot, too cold, hates the crowd, hates the rides...Melanie called him on it.

"I was thinking about going but forget about it if we go to the concert," he said.

"You have no intention of doing neither; you're just trying to guilt me for wanting to do something as a couple. I'll agree to the park and when the time comes, you'll find a reason not to go."

"What? Are you accusing me of manipulating you?" he said, anger building in his voice. "Well, congratulations. You finally figured me out. Took what, fourteen years?"

"I knew it. I didn't question it because I didn't want you to fly into a rage. I've had enough, and I'm sick of it. I feel like a prisoner," Melanie cried.

Rob began walking toward her. "You do huh? How about me? You wouldn't be living in that nice house or drive that nice van if it wasn't for me working day and night here! If I left this all today, you wouldn't have a clue how to take care of yourself. See how well you'd do on your own. You'd die."

"Try me!"

"You..." Rob brought his arm back to slug her hard.

The sound of Kayla's phone breaks Melanie's thoughts. She left it on the counter when she rushed off to school this morning. It's an incoming text from Nick. Melanie reads it.

Nick: *Hey, how r u doing? Just ignore those girls at school. They're skanks. Been thnkn a lot about u l8ly. Miss u.* (three heart emojis and a happy face emoji blowing a kiss).

Melanie deletes it. She knows she shouldn't. *Kayla's just too young for that.*

Melanie remembers what it was like in school. They make fun of you for anything. It's no picnic. You're either the bully or the victim. It's nice Kayla finally has friends, but she needs to cool it with that boy. He's older than her. Maybe now that she'll be in high school, she'll meet a nice young man in her class.

*

After class during the first week of school, Kayla opens her locker to retrieve a Math book. The boy at the next locker eyes her up and down. *Creep.*

"Hey, aren't you the girl with a meat market in her garage?" The creep smiles with a mouth full of braces.

She turns to ignore him when she is surrounded by three other guys, laughing, and leering at her. They won't let her pass.

"I got some meat for you." He grabs his crotch. Kayla wants to kick him there in the worst way, but she only bows her head trying her best to avoid them. *God, I hate this school!*

The guy with braces grabs her by the arm when he is elbowed by one of his friends.

"Dag, it's him...the serial killer."

Kayla lifts her head. A tall skinny guy wearing all black, including black gloves is approaching them. "A serial killer?" *Could this be the guy who made my dad disappear?*

The boys move away from her. Dag lets her go. He answers her in a harsh whisper. "He's a real creep. He's always talkin' bout killin' us. He collects guns."

Kayla brings her hand to cover her mouth—not in fear, but laughter. "Dag? Is that short for Dagwood? I never heard of..."

"Shut up!" He hisses. He slams his locker shut and joins his friends down the hall.

"They bug me too. Don't worry, tomorrow they'll be dead."

Kayla jumps. The boy in black is right behind her. He nods his head bringing out a gloved hand to her. She hesitantly shakes his hand.

"I'm Raven, the good beast who will destroy all bad creatures."

"Um," Kayla swallows back her fear, curiosity overpowering it. "Kayla. Nice to meet you?"

"There is a beast in all of us. We are given the choice to do what is right or wrong. I choose right. My calling is to destroy all that is wrong." Raven stares down at Kayla. His deep-set eyes give her goose bumps.

His irises are so dark she believes he's wearing black contact lenses.

"Have you, uh...destroyed anyone yet?" Raven doesn't answer her. He glides down the hallway and enters a classroom when tardy bell rings. Kayla stands at her still open locker in a daze. *He could be the killer. I gotta tell Principal Clark about this.*

When the principal confronts the boy, he denies any of it. They search his locker and find nothing. Now, she's afraid Raven will target her for ratting on him. She keeps feeling like someone is watching her.

Kayla tells her mother about it, and she is enraged.

"That's it. I'm not going to let my daughter live in fear of anyone. I lived like that for far too long. I'm not going to let it happen to you."

*

The next morning, Melanie takes Kayla to school. She goes to breakfast while her mother talks to the principal, Mr. Clark. He says he can't suspend the boy on hearsay. Kayla is the only one who heard him.

"Kayla heard him. She never lies."

"What lies every time it opens its mouth?" Mr. Clark asks.

"What?"

"A teenager," he laughs. Melanie doesn't think it's funny. He's being a jerk. She is done.

No man is going to be a jerk to me or my daughter ever again.

"Kayla doesn't need this abuse...from anyone! I am pulling her out of this stink-hole of a district. I'm going to home school her, and she'll learn much more than you..."

Loud popping sounds erupt from the hall. Melanie knows that sound—a gun!

Mr. Clark immediately gets on the intercom and shouts "Lock down."

Melanie peers around the corner to see a young man. He matches Kayla's description of the boy who scared her. He is carrying a rifle and pointing it toward the students at breakfast. *Kayla is in there!* Melanie wants to run and tackle the shooter, yet she could get herself killed in the process. She must remain calm. She takes a deep breath and realizes what must be done.

Mr. Clark is hiding under his desk. Melanie holds a finger to her lips for quiet. She silently pulls a nine milli-meter pistol from her purse. The shooter is standing in the doorway of the cafeteria reloading. She points her gun at him and steadies herself.

"You feel lucky, punk?" Melanie shouts. It wasn't what she wanted to say, it just came out.

The shooter spins to face her. He raises his rifle...shaking, when suddenly, he is tackled to the floor by Mr. Moses, the custodian. Melanie quickly grabs the shooter's rifle. Mr. Clark calls the police. Only Dag is injured. He has been shot in the shoulder, missing a major blood vessel by an inch. Melanie searches for Kayla. She is hiding under a table when she sees her mother. She runs into her arms. They hold each other tight.

The boy had been relentlessly teased and his target was the bullies. He doesn't have a father and his mother is in rehab after a drug overdose. He was living with his abusive grandparents, and stole the gun from his grandfather, who has a whole arsenal of weapons.

Melanie believes Rob was a bully in school. It makes her wonder how much better her life would have been had she realized it and never married him.

Melanie is going to pull Kayla out of school. She doesn't need the worry, and besides, Melanie can't run the business alone. She can't trust anyone else to work for her. She's determined to prove she can be a success.

Kayla is glad. She hates that school. She'll do better at home away from those morons. "Mom? Do you think that guy, Raven, could be the one who made those guys disappear?"

"Honey, his name isn't Raven...it's Bradley Miles. Being threatening was the only way he could cope. Yes, he shot someone, but his motive was revenge. I'm sure he didn't know the men who disappeared. They were all much older."

"You didn't talk to him. He was really disturbed. I think he could have done it."

"He's in good hands now. I'm sure he'll be taken care of. I can't imagine they would let someone as mentally tortured as he is rot in jail."

Kayla studies her hands lost in thought. *Will he rot in jail? Will any more guys disappear? How can they help someone like Raven? How?*

A Witness

Nick is walking home after a football scrimmage. The coach got them all pizza after the game and now it's getting dark. The air is still comfortable, especially with the cloud cover keeping the evening's warmth closer to the ground, but they also block the moonlight.

Nick is uneasy walking home after dark. He keeps thinking back to the time something followed him home.

I'll be glad when I get my driver's license next month. He stops and nervously glances about—nothing, not even the sound of the night crickets. *Click, click, click,* nails to cement. He quickens his stride. *Click tappity, click tappity, click tappity.*

He bolts, running full tilt toward home. The sound is getting louder, panting close behind. He leaps to the stoop of his home and works the door when he is slammed against it. A guttural growl blends with his heart pounding in his ears, Nick slowly turns around. Facing him are huge, sharp, white teeth surrounded by the face of a bear...but it isn't a bear. It has pointed ears and a slender black panther-like body. Its bushy tail flicks while glaring at him with glowing yellow eyes. Reared up on its hind legs, it presses a paw, talons extended, against his chest, piercing it. Nick winces in pain praying for his life.

The beast opens its maw of teeth leaning toward Nick when,

"Oh, my Gawd, Nick, what is that?" It's Sarah, on her way home from cheerleading.

The creature turns and drops to all fours. Sarah screams. Nick falls to the floor. It makes a high-pitched screech like an injured baby and bounds away from them into the brush. Sarah runs to Nick, helps him up and both fall into the house. Sarah locks the doors.

Suddenly, there is a *rush-brrr* sound like a bottle rocket.

"That monster makes that noise. I heard it before," Nick pants.

"Are you alright?" Sarah asks, helping Nick remove his T-shirt.

"I...I think so." He recoils at five puncture wounds to his chest. "Was it a panther?"

Sarah swivels her head toward the door and nods. "I think so. I never saw a panther in the wild before."

"This isn't the wild. It must have escaped from somewhere." Nick touches his chest.

"They're bleeding. I'll get some band-aids," Sarah rushes out of the living room to retrieve some.

He sucks in a breath from pain. "I think I'm gonna need some stitches!"

After Nick's parents take him to the ER, he receives two stitches to each wound and antibiotics. The police are called, and Nick tells them what happened. It doesn't take long for the whole town to hear about the panther. The police suspect it has something to do with the disappearances. There is now a city-wide curfew. No one is to go outside after dark until the creature is caught.

Uncle Mike, worried for Kayla and Melanie's safety, asks them to stay at his house. Melanie flatly refuses. She isn't going to close the shop even for a day. The zoos count on her too much. Kayla wants to go. She believes that it's someone, not the panther responsible for the missing men. She was taking out the garbage behind the house last week when she noticed a tarp covering up something big. Her parents have a smoker in the yard for smoking meat like turkey and sausage. There's wood under the tarp, but the shape under it was much larger than the wood needed for the smoker. Kayla had to see what it was. She lifted a corner of it. It was a motorcycle. She thinks it was Mumert's. She couldn't be too sure because it was dark when she saw it, but it had the same flat black paint on it. Maybe her father killed him and hid his bike there. Kayla felt he was watching her right then. She ran and told her mother what she had found. Melanie came out with her to look. She too peered toward the edges of the lawn. Her eyes couldn't focus to the impeding dark. The clouds were hiding the crescent moon. Her mother didn't speak for what seemed like forever.

Melanie told her not to tell anyone, that her father is trying to pin the murders on her. Kayla wants to run, but her mother is so determined to be successful at the shop that she will risk their lives for it. Her daughter has no choice.

*

Melanie finishes cleaning up the shop and loading the van for a shipment when she immediately stops what she is doing and listens. Outside the wall of her shop, leaves disturbed by the shuffling of feet. The sound moves toward the back of the building. Melanie quickly puts her back against the wall beside the door and does her best to quietly turn the dead bolt to lock it--her breath in shallow pants. She grabs her gun. The doorknob turns one way then another. Her adrenaline rises.

BAM, BAM, BAM! Banging on the door—Melanie faces the window ready to blow its head off.

It's Detective Billings. She quickly stows her gun under her apron into the waist of her jeans. Melanie opens the door.

"You gave me such a start," She gasps, hand upon her chest.

"I surely didn't mean to startle you. I was just nosing around a bit. You heard about Nick Michaels?" Detective Billings asks.

Melanie shakes her head *no*. "What does this shop have to do with Nick Michaels? All I know is that he's a friend of my daughter. What about him?" The detective has interrupted her busy day.

"Well, ma'am," he smiles kindly, "The young man was assaulted by some kind of animal."

Melanie's hand covers her mouth in surprise.

"Since you have a meat shop, I thought maybe it could roam here."

"We...we live an hour away from his family.

I don't think an animal could smell my shop that far away." Melanie sniffs. "Is the young man, uh Nick...alright?"

"He just needed a few stitches. From his description this animal is nothing to mess with. Sounds like one crazy beast. Who knows where it's gonna roam? Lotta folks want to hunt for it. We put some measures in place for a controlled search. It probably escaped from one of those tiger zoos. We don't need any accidental deaths, now do we...and besides, I haven't ruled out homicide.

Is your husband still missing?"

"Yes, he hasn't been here for months. I still have your card. I told you I would give you a call if I saw him. What are you insinuating? You think I have something..."

"As I said, I'm just nosing around. I'm not insinuating anything. I can understand why you don't want to hear from your husband if he ran off, but I must cover all bases. I saw your van. Do you own any other vehicles?"

Melanie shakes her head, *no.*

"None that maybe you park else where's?"

"None." She grits her teeth.

"Mind if I look around a bit more?"

Seriously? Should I ask for a search warrant? "No, that's fine. Be my guest."

Detective Billings looks around and in the back of the van, the walk-in freezer, and the house. He completely misses the motorcycle under the tarp, and Melanie isn't going to tell him about it either. He's wasted enough of her time. "So, what does this animal look like? I should know what to look for."

"It's a black panther...only twice as big, with a long, fluffy tail."

Melanie begins to chuckle. "Oh, a big mean creature with a fluffy tail?"

"I guess so."

Melanie laughs out loud.

"This isn't funny, Ma'am."

Melanie doesn't know what got into her. She just can't help herself. It reminds her of a cartoon. The prey yelling, "Help me, help me" in a little high voice while a big kitty cat with a fluffy tail has it pinned against a door. Nick probably deserved it.

She calls her brother, Mike, after the detective leaves. Again, he begs her to go stay with him awhile. *Right. I'd much rather stay here and take my chances than to go there and watch them all go gaga over the baby, and Sheila and I would do all of the work while Mike sits and watches TV all night. No thank you.* Kayla is going to have a day off for parent-teacher conferences on Friday. Melanie decides she can have a long weekend with them. She plans to pull her from school then. She will be safer. Melanie vows she will do whatever it takes for her daughter to grow up in a place where she won't be afraid of saying or doing the wrong thing. She'll grow up beautiful and confident in who she is, with no man to tear her down. *Mike better watch her as though it depends on his life.*

*

Jerry's Pa is watching the news about the creature.

"It's some kind of animal let loose."

"Mmm," Ma hums, reading a magazine on the sofa.

"Could still be an alien. We don't know what they look like. They could be somethin' that looks like a bear mixed up with a panther," Pa claims in awe.

"Ain't no more panthers in North Carolina. I told you," Ma answers.

"Jus' like always, you ain't listenin' to me! You're worthless as our son. Them aliens are some kind of mixed-up animal, and no one can go outside." Pa's face is turning red from frustration.

"All that excitement is in Rockwell, not here!" Ma yells.

"You're gonna make me get up from this chair and slap some sense into ya! Son of a ..." He struggles to get out of his chair, straining forward to get the footrest down when Jerry runs into the room.

"Pa! Don't hurt Ma no more!" Jerry cries.

Pa pulls a pistol from the band of his pants and points it at Jerry. "Oh yeah? Ma may have put you into this world, but I sure as hell can take you out! You shouldn't a been born anyways."

Jerry bows his head and steps back. "I'm sorry Pa."

"I'm sorry Pa," Pa mimics. "Boy, you are stupider than shit." He puts the pistol back. "Get me a beer." "And git back into your room," Ma yells at Jerry.

Jerry quickly obeys.

At Uncle Mike's

Kayla is thrilled to get away and spend three days with Uncle Mike, Aunt Sheila, little Noah, Sarah, and best of all, Nicky. Her mother takes her, but she doesn't stay. She says she has too much work to do which makes Kayla wonder if she should be home helping her, but she won't get to see everyone again till Christmas.

Little Noah is precious. He can sit up a little and he smiles. He's eight weeks old already. It seems like only a few weeks ago Kayla's life was normal. Her father working in the shop. Her mother helping him, and she went to school--just day to day living. Kayla even misses being teased by her father. She misses his tricks--like sticking his missing finger up his nose. Tears begin to well in Kayla's eyes when Noah smiles a huge happy baby smile. It is the sweetest smile on the planet. Kayla lifts his little T-shirt and blows raspberries on his belly. It makes the funniest fart sound. His arms and legs wave about in excitement. He smells like baby powder. Aunt Sheila picks him up for his feeding and goes into the bedroom.

A soft head nudges itself under Kayla's arm. It's Shep. She hugs him around his neck. Tears find their track down her cheeks and over her lips tasting their salty wetness. Shep licks them away. He's such a sweet dog-and smart. He follows Uncle Mike everywhere and he quickly learned how to open the fridge and get him a beer. Aunt Sheila isn't happy about that because now Shep gets in there and eats leftovers. Uncle Mike likes it because he hates leftovers. Kayla laughs thinking about it.

Sometimes Shep has his bouts of sadness. He'll sit for hours staring out of the living room window and whines. It's like he's waiting for Mumert to come home.

Uncle Mike says he'll look for him when things calm down.

Kayla decides to tell Uncle Mike about the motorcycle under the tarp. He's surprised to hear that Mumert's bike is at their house. He calls Melanie. No answer. He tries again an hour later. Mike needs to know what is going on.

"Hello?"

"Mel. You finally answered."

"I'm busy. Is Kayla okay?"

"Yeah, she's fine, but she just told me Mumert's motorcycle is stashed there. What the hell is going on?" There is a long pause on the other end. "Mel?"

"Sigh, I don't know. It appeared not long after Rob left. I think it belonged to him. He left it there for some reason. It's not your friend, Mumert's bike. I'm sure of it."

"I didn't know Rob rode a bike."

"Well, you two aren't exactly buddies, so how would you know? He started riding a year ago. I think he left it there to make the police think I have something to do with the disappearances, the asshole."

"Man, we gotta find Rob. Everything is getting too freaky."

"Rob doesn't want to be found. He's probably on some tropical island with someone half his age. I'm stuck with all the bills and work."

"Kayla says she believes he could kill someone."

Melanie draws his name out with a long breath, "Mike, she's a kid with a wild imagination. I'm safe. No boogy man...or monster is after us. Relax. Listen, I gotta go. A shipment just came in. Good meat can't wait."

"Be careful...okay?"

"Yep. No problem. I'll call you later, bye."

Silence on his phone. Melanie didn't even wait for him to say *Goodbye. Something is wrong with her.*

*

Sarah arrives at Uncle Mike's for a sleepover with Kayla. Kayla tries to call Nick with no luck. Sarah tells her about the panther that hurt him.

"This is all so screwed up. First, I think my dad is a killer and now some freaky escaped panther? So what? He doesn't want to come over because he might become cat-food?" Kayla asks.

"That panther was huge...and scary. I don't blame him," Sarah says.

"Well, you're here."

"That's 'cause I came during daylight. Nicky can't come till after dark."

"What? The creature is only active after dark?"

"I think so," Sarah shrugs.

"Let's sneak over to Nicky's so I can talk to him."

"What about the panther?"

"I'm more afraid of my dad than some hairy animal. Come on, Nicky's only about a few blocks away. No one will miss us."

"Yeah, let's do it," Sarah smiles. "Fuck you, Mr. Panther, you raggedy old thing!" she shouts holding up both her middle fingers. Kayla laughs.

When they arrive at Nick's the girls notice a light on in an upstairs window. They hope its Nick's room. They pick up pebbles and toss them at his window. They guess right. Nick opens it.

"Shit, it's you," he whispers.

Kayla tosses a rock at him and misses. "Well, that's some, how dee do,"

"No, I mean, I'm glad to see you...but"

"Just get down here."

He shuts his window and sneaks silently out the back door, glancing all around him.

"What's with you? It's just an animal."

Nick lifts his T shirt over his chest. The stitches, still fresh, knitting his wounds, "An animal that did this."

"Oh, my gawd! Geez, I'm sorry."

"It's okay. We gotta take this seriously. It could be out here right now."

Kayla gazes into Nick's eyes. "I'm out here right now. No...no cat will keep me away."

"Come here." He takes her by the arm and pulls her toward the hedge. "Shhh."

"I'll keep a look out," Sarah says.

Hidden in the shadow of the bushes Nick

embraces Kayla. He isn't wearing Axe this time. It's his natural smell. She buries her face into his neck. It smells like he has been outside in the fall air all day--woodsy with a whiff of wet grass after a rain. Nick takes her face into his hands and kisses Kayla on the lips. His lips soft yet firm and slightly parted--smooth, silky heaven. She could have kissed him all night. He hugs her tightly. She's light-headed.

"Listen, go home. I want you to be safe, okay?" Nick's gorgeous brown eyes with big awesome lashes are gazing at her. Kayla would've agreed to anything at that moment.

"Okay."

Suddenly, they hear barking from a distance.

"It's Shep!" Kayla cries.

"Go!"

She grabs Sarah and runs toward the sound. It's Uncle Mike calling. Kayla and Sarah stop when they see him and Shep. They stumble into a walk doing their best to look nonchalant.

Uncle Mike runs up to the girls out of breath. Shep jumps up on Kayla and licks her face.

"Where were you? You had us all scared. It's past curfew!" he pants.

"We were just taking a walk," Sarah says.

"Well, this is no damn time to be takin' a walk. God only knows what's out here. I couldn't live with myself if you disappeared. I feel sick just thinkin' about it," There is a glimmer of tears in his eyes. Kayla's posture slumps, chin to her chest. She didn't realize he would be so upset.

"I'm sorry, Uncle Mike."

"It's okay," he waves. "I'm glad you two are back. Don't do that to us again."

"I won't," Kayla promises...*except maybe to see Nicky again.*

Back at the house in her room Sarah and Kayla tell each other horror stories.

"Did you hear the one about the big toe?" Kayla asks Sarah.

She shakes her head, still freaked out about the sight of the panther pinning Nick.

"True story," Kayla continues. "There was this guy lost in the Uwharrie Forest. He was there for days and was starving when he came across a big toe lying among the leaves. He picked it up expecting to find a body, but there was none. He was so hungry he decided to cook it over a fire where he was camping."

"He had a fire?" Sarah asks. "I thought he was lost."

"He was, but he knew how to make a fire."

"Well, if he knew how to make a fire couldn't he make like smoke signals to get help?"

"I guess. Maybe he didn't think of that."

"Did he have water? You die in only a few days without water."

"Gawd, just let me tell the story. There's lots of water in the forest...okay?"

"Okay," Sarah is thoughtful, "I was just wondering..."

"Anyway! He ate the toe."

"Oh, gross! What if that panther ate those guys?"

"What?"

"They can't find the bodies. Maybe it ate them...like maybe your dad too."

"Sarah, that's horrible. Ugh! Now I'm too disgusted to finish the story."

"No, no, finish it. I'm sorry. I just wonder...that's all. So, he ate the toe and...?"

The thought of it is revolting to Kayla. It all just doesn't seem real--like her story.

"Come on," Sarah pleads. "Please?"

Kayla lets out a deep sigh and continues. "That night, he heard a voice call out, *Where's my toe?* He sat up and thought that maybe it was just indigestion, but this time it was louder, *Where's my toe?* He stood up and tried to peer into the woods. He heard footsteps over the leaves. A branch snapped, when he heard the voice even louder, *Where's my toe?*"

Sarah swallows in fear.

"You got it!" Kayla grabs Sarah's foot. She jumps, almost falling off of the bed.

"That was bad. I think I peed myself a little," she laughs.

Later, lying in bed, Kayla wonders if the panther ate her father.

*

The next morning after Sarah goes home, Uncle Mike takes Kayla to a gun range. He tells her she should be prepared to protect herself. She can't wait to learn how to shoot a gun.

"What if your dad is the killer? What if you knew if you didn't kill him, he would kill you?" Uncle Mike asks.

"No way would my dad kill me."

"Okay, what if you knew he would kill more people and the only way to stop him would be to kill him?"

"He's not killing people," Kayla defends. "The panther got them. I could shoot it if I have to."

"What if your father was killing your mother?" A huge lump forms in Kayla's throat, tears well in her eyes. It would be the hardest, most horrible decision of her life. She can't answer him.

"I'm sorry. I didn't mean to upset you. You don't have to do this." Uncle Mike parks the car but leaves the engine running. "I want you to be ready for anything. I love you...as my niece I don't know how I could live with myself if you got hurt."

"I want to learn. I want to be able to protect myself. I pray it won't be from my dad."

Mike turns off the engine and pats Kayla.

"It's my prayer too, K K."

The instructor at the range gives her a Ruger 22 caliber pistol. Kayla is scared to hold it at first, but when she does, it feels comfortable in her hand and not heavy. She aims at the target the way the instructor tells her to and fires. The recoil isn't bad at all, but she misses the bullseye. He tells her to take a few deep breaths and fire as she is exhaling. She does, and BAM hits the bullseye. It feels totally awesome. She misses a lot, but Uncle Mike promises to take her to the range every time she visits.

Kayla has a fantastic time and asks Uncle Mike for a Ruger for Christmas. He hands her a box before they leave the gun range. It's the Ruger! He tells her to be safe with it and that it might stop someone, but it won't kill them. He asks Kayla not to mention it to Aunt Sheila. She hates guns. Kayla figures she better not say anything to her mom either.

When they return to the house, Kayla runs up to her room and sends a selfie holding her Ruger in a cute pose with the message: *I got ur back, boi!* to Nick.

He doesn't text her back.

Her mother shows up at Uncle Mike's on Sunday in time for brunch. She is grey looking, and she has bags under her eyes like she hasn't slept. Aunt Sheila asks if she feels alright. She says she's working too hard and begins to help Sheila prepare the dishes.

"Mel don't worry about that. You haven't seen baby Noah yet." She shooshes Melanie away.

Kayla takes her mother's hand. "Come on, I'll take you to him."

Shep rouses from his spot in front of the crib when they enter Noah's room. His hackles rise, and he growls at Melanie. She takes a step forward. Shep snaps at her and barks.

Kayla never saw Shep act that way before. "Sorry, Mom, Shep is protective." She runs over to the dog, takes him by the collar and leads him to the bathroom.

She shuts the door. Shep continues to bark and snap, but now a door is between him and Melanie.

Melanie eyes her daughter. "Protective, huh?"

The look on her face is the same as when Kayla tries to feed her a line of bull. "He's a good dog."

Kayla's mother stands at the crib staring at the baby. Her face shows nothing...she continues to look worn, old.

"Mom? You can pick him up. He won't break." She smiles, her mother doesn't.

Melanie leans over and picks up Noah. She holds him like a sack of potatoes. He seems to be nothing to her. Shep continues his barking. The whole scene is disturbing to Kayla...especially when her mother talks to the baby.

"You will grow up to be kind. I'll make sure you don't hurt your mother or wife or daughter or any other woman in your life. If you do, you will cease to exist to me."

"Um, okay Mom, let's put Noah back. He needs to finish his nap." Kayla rushes to take Noah from her mother's grip. Shep is getting ballistic.

Melanie releases Noah and seems to sleep walk into the next room. After putting Noah back in bed, she lets Shep out of the bathroom and shuts the bedroom door. He sniffs through the bars of the crib at Noah. Kayla pets the dog to calm him down. "What's the matter, boy? It was just my mom. She won't hurt anybody." Shep growls. Noah giggles.

Melanie enters the kitchen. "You shouldn't have a dog like that around your child. He almost bit me."

Mike's eyebrows rise in surprise. "Shep? He's the sweetest, goofiest dog I've ever known."

"Not around me."

Kayla enters. "I don't know what got into him. He's okay now."

"Maybe you should have him put down before he hurts somebody. Even if he doesn't bite the baby, if he bites someone like the mailman, you'll have a huge lawsuit on your hands." Melanie pulls out a chair and sits at the table.

Mike stands at his chair frozen in disbelief. "I'm not going to do that. The dog belongs to my best friend who's one of the missing guys. He loves that boy. The dog never leaves his side. You must have startled him." Sheila places sandwiches and a bowl of potato salad on the table. "We'll keep a close eye on the dog, Mel. I understand your concern."

Melanie stretches and cracks her neck. Kayla can tell her mother is aggravated. "I'm sure you do."

This isn't her mother at all. Something is terribly wrong with her, but Kayla can't put her finger on it. *Would the flu make her act this way? Maybe she shouldn't have held Noah. Maybe that's it. Shep sensed she was too sick to hold the baby.*

Sheila sits next to Melanie. She gently places her hand on hers. "Can you eat? I hope you don't have a fever. Maybe you should go lie down."

Melanie jerks her hand away. "I'm fine. I told you. I'm just tired. I've been doing the job of four people. I can't find anyone qualified to work at the shop. This is a good time to tell you...I'm pulling Kayla from school so she can help me out."

Mike's hands fall to both sides of his plate. "What are you talking about, Mel?"

"She is safer at home with me, and I can't run the shop myself anymore."

Sheila joins the argument. "Kayla needs to be in school. She needs to be around other children her age."

"I'll home school her."

"Mom, I need to go to school here."

"Mel, you don't have time to work at the shop and home school."

"I'll just learn how to butcher old meat." Dread and fear of doing nothing but working in the cold garage with frozen animals stripped of their skin causes Kayla to begin sobbing. "You and Dad adopted me for free labor!"

"We did nothing of the sort."

"You need to hire help. You're running yourself into the ground."

"Why can't I stay here and go to school with Sarah?" A plead for mercy.

"Stop! All of you. Just stop. Kayla is MY daughter and what I say, goes. I've already pulled her out. She can return in a year or so...when everything is back to normal," Melanie is adamant.

"What is normal...Mom?"

Mike sits, glaring at his sister. "I should have a say in this."

She glares hard back at him. "You have no rights. I'm doing it for our well-being. This work will pay off in the future and Kayla will be happy and live a good life.

It is all up to me, and only me."

After what seems to be an eternity to Kayla, Uncle Mike picks up his sandwich and begins eating in silence.

Noah is fussing in the other room. Aunt Sheila stands to retrieve the baby. Kayla dries her eyes on her napkin and picks at the salad with her fork.

Her mother hasn't touched her food. "I promise I will work with her studies every day from seven to ten a.m. and some evenings. Sound good?"

Uncle Mike grumbles with a mouth full of food in agreement.

"Does it have to be seven a.m.?" Kayla asks.

"Yes," her mother's simple answer.

Chapter 10

Bodies

Kayla is quiet all the way home and keeps her head down looking at her cell phone. *Still nothing from Nick.* She turns on the car radio.

The news comes on. It is normal information about traffic and weather until the DJ begins to tell the listening audience the evening curfew is continuing.

"If you must go out, travel with another person. A body has been discovered. He has been identified as Richard..." Melanie turns off the radio.

"You don't need to hear that."

Kayla's mind buzzes with questions. "I still think it's Dad. Richard who? Where are the rest of the bodies? If it is that panther, why is it all men? Did they all die? If Dad or that animal tries to do anything to us, I'll shoot them. I've got a gun and I'll protect you."

"What?" her mother yells.

Crap. "Uh, Uncle Mike bought me a gun for protection."

"That goober did, did he?" She is hot.

"He took me to a shooting range to learn how to use it safely. It's all good, Mom."

"It is, huh? What kind is it?"

"A Ruger 22."

"That won't protect us. It'll only do a little more damage than a pellet gun. Hit your father with that and he'd turn into a freight train heading for your throat."

"It wouldn't slow him down?"

"No, that's why you can't have it. You're going to give it to me, and I'll put it in a safe place."

"But Mom..."

"I'll teach you on a much better gun."

I blew it! She'll never show me how to shoot. She'll never have time. Kayla decides she isn't going to talk to her mother the rest of the day. *She can do whatever--and she didn't even answer my questions.*

At home, Kayla runs straight to her room after handing her mother the gun. She is so angry she wants to shoot her with it. Of course, she doesn't, but her mother makes Kayla mad enough to. Melanie leaves Kayla dinner outside her bedroom door--hot dogs, coleslaw, and chips. Kayla tries to text Nick again, no luck. She eats her food and goes to bed. Normally she loves a hot dog with a big scoop of coleslaw on top. Today, it has no taste to her. She has no taste in what she will be doing instead of going to school. *Oh joy, I get to chop and grind animals.*

Gee I love my life...NOT.

*

"Lookit that. Look!" Jerry's father yells while pointing at the TV. "There's a picture of the big cat."

Jerry and his mother run into the living room to see a photo beside the newscaster. "Well, I'll be a monkey's aunt. Look at that! It's a panther. Pa, turn up the TV," Ma orders.

The newswoman reads with her serious monotone. "This is a photo of the creature taken by a local resident. It was discovered in the vicinity Richard Greene was found. It was apparent he had been attacked by the animal believed to be an unusually large panther which makes this an extremely dangerous situation. There are traps and trained hunters looking for it. It is strongly advised to remain indoors as much as possible until the animal is caught."

"I knew it! I told you we're being invaded," Pa shouts leaning forward in his chair.

"It's just a panther. They don't run around attackin' folks," Ma swipes at the air just behind Pa's head.

Pa stands up out of his chair. He paces. Jerry doesn't know what to think. It looked like a big black house cat in the photo.

"No one is to go outside. I ain't mowin' knowin' that thing is out there."

"Pa, the yard is surrounded by an eight-foot chain-link fence," The grimace on Ma's face is the same as when she finds a mountain of dishes in the sink.

Jerry's usually the one in trouble when he sees that look. "It could easily jump over it. Look at me," Pa says rubbing his colossal gut. "I'd feed that thing for a week! We don't have to get groceries. We have enough canned food and vegetables in the cellar to last at least a month.

We'll be safe. I'm gonna batten down the hatches."

Jerry's father moves forward, wincing in pain. He sits down clutching at his chest.

"I don't think its indigestion this time, Maude. I'm havin' a...heart attack," he gasps in agony. He tries to take a deep breath. "Feels like the...frigerator sittin' on my chest. Call 911," he wheezes.

Jerry's feet are frozen to the floor in fear and panic. His mother quickly runs into the kitchen and picks up the receiver of the wall phone to call for help. As she talks, Jerry forces himself to move. He stands by her side, heart caught in this throat. A dial tone's high pitch drones on. Ma tells it their address.

Pa leans back in his easy chair gasping for breath...until it is gone.

Ma goes on with her business making dinner.

Jerry stands over his father gawking at him. He can't process in his mind what his mother has done.

Pa remains dead in his chair for several days before a decision is made.

"We have to get rid of him, he's startin' to smell." Ma fans at the air walking past Pa.

"Call 9...1...1?" Jerry asks.

"No. No one is to know Pa has passed away. We need his disability money. The payments'll stop if they know he's dead."

"But Ma..." Jerry tries to protest.

"Hush. You do what I say, or I'll beat the livin' shit outta you."

Jerry drags his pa to the basement—his head making a sickening thump every time it hit a step. He tries to stuff him into a garbage bag, but his father is bigger than thirty-nine gallons. Ma rolls up the dining room area rug and gives Jerry plastic wrap.

"Roll him up in the rug and wrap it all in the plastic wrap. It'll hold the stink in," Ma orders. "Then, tuck'm under the stairs."

Jerry lays the rug out on the basement floor and rolls his father into it. He's nauseous and dizzy. He must do what his mother tells him to. He tries to wind the plastic wrap around the rug, but his father is too heavy to get the wrap properly under him. Ma stomps down the stairs. "You dumbass, do I have to teach you everything? Give me that!" She reaches out and jerks the plastic wrap away from Jerry. She orders, "Unroll him." Jerry obeys. "Roll him offa the rug, idiot!" Jerry obeys.

Ma tugs the rug off to one side. She pulls out a long sheet of plastic wrap and places it carefully on the floor. She repeats the process until the wrap covers the same square feet as the rug. "Pick it up." She lifts one side of the rug, Jerry the other. They place the rug on top of the plastic. She points at Pa. "Now finish it, fool."

Ma clops up the basement stairs, Jerry pushes Pa onto the rug rolling him up. He does his best to seal the ends. He drags his pa underneath the stairs. Later, in the bathtub, Jerry tries to scrub death off of his skin. Tears mix in with the soap and water. He's ignorant about good and bad, but what he's done feels bad...so very bad. He rinses out the tub, refills it and soaks in the clean water. He isn't washed. He can still feel his father on him.

*

Melanie wakes Kayla from a deep slumber early the next morning. She was having a good dream. She and Nick were married, and Noah was their baby. Nick was pushing Noah on a swing and Noah could talk really well. He was saying, "Thank you, Daddy. You're the best," then Kayla nuzzled Nicky's neck and smelled his natural grass after a rain smell and...BOOM her mother is shaking her awake. *Ugh!*

"It's time to go to work."

After a quick breakfast, Kayla puts on a sweater. The morning air has a chill. Halloween is going to be the next week. Kayla hopes her mother will take her to

Uncle Mike's. Sarah's having a big party and Nick is going to be there. She hasn't given up on him yet...especially after that last luscious kiss.

Kayla goes into the shop. Melanie has the saw going. It is obvious her mother has fallen behind on her work. Meat is everywhere. It's a mess. Her mother never left a mess before. Melanie is working on a frozen hind quarter of beef that is strapped in the hoist. She instructs Kayla to hold the leg so that it doesn't flop to the floor. It's heavy. Kayla hefts it to the steel table while Melanie carves another piece. Kayla then preps the shipping boxes, prints labels, and helps her mother with the ribs. It's hard work.

Melanie turns on the grinder to make hamburger out of the by-products and tells her daughter there is more in the chest freezer. Kayla lifts the lid and begins pulling out tongues, ears, hoofs, and hearts when she comes across a knee--two knees. They are human knees. She feels along the legs moving packages out of the way. The knees are attached to a torso, then one arm. The other arm is shredded all the way up to the shoulder. Kayla is cold.

Her chest begins to hurt because she isn't breathing. Her mind spins--her world spins. Her mouth dry as the desert. Kayla can't speak. She can't scream when she sees him. His face is frozen and terribly contorted, but she can tell who it is...her father. She falls to her knees.

"Kayla!" she hears her mother cry out before blacking out.

When Kayla awakes, she's praying she was just having a bad nightmare. Her mother is on the floor, sobbing and rocking her in her arms.

"I'm sorry, I'm sorry," she keeps repeating. "Your father...your father was a bad man. He was abusive. He put me down every day and when the accident happened,

I didn't run for help. I...I watched him die," she weeps. "I was sick of his manipulations and when he swung at me, I deflected his fist. My adrenalin must have been flying because I knocked his fist into the running meat grinder. He screamed for me to hit the emergency shut off right there beside him. I was afraid that if I hit it, he would grab me and kill me. He was panicking and flopping around it, missing the button until the grinder was at his shoulder...when he hit it. He slumped to the floor reaching for me with his good hand making a fist. At that moment I lost my mind. I yelled at him. I told him we weren't going to be tortured by him anymore. I told him that he was a horrible man and a bully. I told him my biggest mistake in life was marrying him. I was so full of fury I didn't think that he was actually dying. When he took his last breath, I decided I couldn't call the police. They would accuse me of murder, take you away from me and we'd lose the business. I didn't know what to do with him then, so I hid him in the freezer. Thank God Detective Billings didn't look there." "What? What am I hearing?" Kayla swallows the urge to throw up.

"Please forgive me, Kayla. I did it for us," Melanie hugs her daughter tight.

A huge numbness rolls over Kayla's being. Her limbs have fallen asleep. Her hands tingle. The blood to them has been cut off.

Her mother lowers her voice to a whisper, "Dying doing what he loves most, working in his shop, is what he would have wanted. We need to process him now."

"No, Mommy...No!" Kayla screams pushing her forcefully away. "He would want to be still alive. That's what Dad would have wanted! We can't...process him."

"Detective Billings might come back and find him. Kayla, darling, your father was a bad man. You know it. He hurt me many times. He was an angry, spiteful monster. He hurt you once and I swore to myself it would never happen again."

"Why would he hurt me? I'm a good girl. Why would he even want to hurt me? You're lying!" "He slammed you into the side of the tub and pulled your arm out of its socket because you had an accident. You were only thirteen months old," Melanie begins to cry, her face in her hands.

Kayla swallows hard--tears finding their way into the corners of her mouth. Her whole life has just changed in the blink of an eye. She wishes she hadn't found him. She wants to run to her mother and soothe her, but she wants to process her father and that's what keeps Kayla frozen in place.

"Kayla," Melanie stands, "You're the best daughter I could ever hope for...pray for. You never once questioned me nor your father, but I really need your help and support now. I can't do it anymore by myself. We'll work together and make this a successful business ourselves."

Kayla remembers Mumert's motorcycle under the tarp out back near the smoker. The way her mother is talking is scary. "Mom, do you know what happened to Mumert?"

Melanie bows her head.

"Mom! You didn't. Please say you didn't kill him," Kayla asks panic rising in her voice. "He was nice. He wasn't a bad man."

"Oh, yes he was. It was an accident. You went right to bed after he led us home. I thanked him and even offered to pay him. He wouldn't leave. He said he wanted his payment another way. Kayla, he grabbed me and began to force himself on me. I somehow convinced him to let me go by telling him that we should have a drink first. I slipped a horse tranquilizer into his drink...ex something. I had some in a syringe in the refrigerator that we use to calm the livestock and squirt it into his beer. I wasn't sure how much of it would be safe for a human. I just wanted him to stop. He was a pretty big guy, so I gave him the whole amount. He downed the whole bottle before he tasted the bitterness.

"He began to molest me again when he got a glazed look in his eyes. He began to drool. He fell over onto the couch. My plan was to drag him out of the house and lock the door. I figured when he came to, he would know it was his cue to go home and leave me alone.

"I drug him out the back door. He was dead weight. He felt cold. I stopped and checked to see if he was breathing. Nothing. I took his pulse--not one beat. I couldn't believe it. Two men down in two weeks. I went into the house trying to figure out what to do with him when I heard something. I thought maybe, by some miracle, Mumert had revived. I looked out the window and saw the panther everyone's been looking for. She sniffed at him, bit down on his head and dragged Mumert into the woods. It was such a relief to be rid of him," Melanie sighs.

"What? You saw it? It's a she?"

"Yes, and I even gave her a name. Grimalkin. It's the name of the witches familiar in Shakespeare's, *Macbeth* who helped them see the future. Our future is going to be wonderful."

There is an uncomfortable silence while Kayla unscrambles it all in her head. *This can't be real.* She can't hold back any longer and throws up on the workshop floor.

"Oh, honey," Her mother begins to cleans it up. "You can't say anything to anyone about this, understand? They'll take me away and you'll never see me again. You'll grow up in foster homes. It would be more horrible than you can imagine. That's what happened to your father and see what it made him?"

THIS is more horrible than Kayla can imagine.

"I'm glad you found your father. I need to tell you more," Melanie tenderly holds Kayla's face in her hands.

"No, Mommy...please...no more," she begs.

"But you must know everything, so you'll understand."

Kayla closes her eyes tightly and prays for help.

*

"Jerry, you need to go to the 7 Eleven and cash your pa's check." He places her tray of food on the TV table in front of her. She hands him a Social Security check. She's watching All My Children while sitting in Pa's easy chair. Jerry holds the check between his fingers like it's covered in some deadly virus. "But..."

"Take it!"

"But I...don't...drive."

"Neither do I, dumbass. You know where it is, walk there." Ma picks up a chicken leg. "I signed Pa's name on the back, so you shouldn't have no trouble." Jerry's in the way of her show. She leans over her tray shoving him aside with her free hand. "Git goin'...and git me a tub a cottage cheese while you're at it."

"Can I...buy...buy a...soda?"

Ma is concentrating on her show while gnawing at the leg. "Whatever."

A guy and some girl are on a bed. Jerry figures they're wrestling under the sheets. He doesn't know why Ma is fascinated the guy always gets the pin. Pride swells in his chest. He is now the man. Jerry slips his bare feet into his dingy grey duct taped tennis shoes. *I'm the man cashing checks.* He opens a cabinet door. Inside is a stack of neatly folded paper grocery sacks. Jerry takes one and tucks it under his arm.

The owner of the 7 Eleven, Mr. Wells, eyes Jerry suspiciously. He has seen him many times with his father, always standing obediently beside him, always buys a soda. Mr. Wells flips the check over to study the signature line. Mr. Pritchard's name is there. "Hi Jerry, never saw you in here without your father. I hope he's well."

Jerry stands at the counter in frozen expectation. The bag is folded in front of the clerk. Jerry is holding a tub of cottage cheese in one hand, a soda in the other. "He...he had...a...heart attack."

Mr. Wells takes a step back in surprise. "Oh my, is he in the hospital?"

Jerry hesitantly nods, his heart thumping in his ears. If he comes home without the money, his mother will beat him senseless with Pa's belt.

Mr. Wells sighs. "I'll have to send him a card. Let him know he has my prayers."

Jerry continues to stare at the empty paper bag.

Mr. Wells follows his gaze. "Oh, yeah," he chuckles. "Nothing bigger than a ten...right?" He opens the register and tucks the check under the drawer containing twenty-dollar bills. He reaches into the other sections pulling out handfuls of cash. He carefully places it in the bag— minus the amount for Jerry's purchase and the check cashing fee. He folds over the top of the bag and hands it to a relieved Jerry. "You know, it'd be a lot easier keeping it in the bank." He closes the drawer of the till.

"We...don't believe...in...in banks."

Mr. Wells tilts his head. Jerry can tell the man is confused. He smiles wide gathering the bag. Mr. Wells hands him a separate package containing the soda and cottage cheese. "Thank...you...Mr. Wells." Jerry waves. pushing the door to head home with Ma's cash.

*

Kayla's mother continues her ghastly onslaught of her side of the story. "I was very angry with Sledge for putting you in danger like that. Those tigers could have killed you! Terrible thought, and Sledge was a terrible man."

"While you were at your Uncle Mike's I went with Sledge for a night delivery to Tiger World. I was yelling at him for putting you in such danger. He laughed. He actually laughed at me. I told him he was fired. He was bending over the tigers teasing them with the meat. I even heard him mumble something about feeding ME to them when one of them swiped at him, slicing his wrist. He ran out of the pen screaming for help.

"I had a first aid kit in the back of the van and hurried to retrieve it when I heard it...a low, mewling sound. Out of the brush crept Grimalkin. I jumped into the van and locked the doors. The tigers huddled in the corner of their cage as far away from her as they could.

"Sledge banged on the window of my van begging to get in, but I was afraid she would attack us both. He bled all over the place. Grimalkin crept toward him. He turned to face her. She sniffed at Sledge, opened her huge jaws, bit into his head, and dragged him into the woods. I was horrified and thrilled at the same time. That creature saved me the work of helping a man who was going to feed me to the tigers. Grimalkin and the tigers knew he was a bad man.

Melanie finishes scrubbing Kayla's throw up. She strolls to the sink to rinse the rag, opens the cabinet for a fresh one and pours cool water onto it. She wrings it out, returns to Kayla, and dabs the coolness on the girl's forehead.

"I thoroughly cleaned the area. I pointed the van's headlights toward the woods where she went in. I had to go in there to be sure there was no sign of Sledge. I couldn't find him. I could have called the police and told them Grimalkin did it, but I was afraid they would search my shop again and find your father. I hadn't decided what to do with him yet...I mean we were married fourteen years."

"Oh, God, Mom...this is horrible. I can't..." Kayla begins.

"The three weeks you spent at Uncle Mike's became a blur in my mind. All I could think of was the sight of that animal taking away Sledge. I was so grateful to Grimalkin that I began leaving meat for her when I fed the tigers. Sometimes I could see her lurking at the edge of the woods. She filled out. I realized her head looked huge because she was so thin. She's the most beautiful panther I have ever seen. My obsession with her caused the work to pile up. I had to get myself together and get things back to normal. The van needed service, so I took it to Richard Greene's garage. It needed an oil change; and I noticed the rear brakes were sticking a bit. Your father always dealt with him. He seemed to do a good job.

'A skinny guy emerged from his shop and headed my way. He had greasy un-kept hair, filthy face, and hands, and he was wearing blue coveralls with the name, *Richard*, embroidered above the front pocket. He had a dumb, *I didn't graduate sixth grade*, look on his face.

'Where's Rob?' Rich asked right away.

"He left."

'Left?'

"Yeah...uh, he left Kayla and me. I got the van," I explained.

'Damn, I wouldn't think he'd leave the van--good utility vehicle.'

"I need it for the shop."

'The shop too?' Rich asked unbelieving. 'Shit, it musta been one heck of a woman,' he mused.

"I didn't appreciate the statement. "Can you just change the oil, and check the brakes, please?" I asked. "They're sticking a little."

'Yeah, sure. Are you leavin' the van?'

"No, I'll wait for it.

'Okay, it might take a while,' he warned.

"I saw a coffee shop across the street. I was in bad need of a break anyway. "That's fine. I'll be at the café across the street," I told him. He said he would call me when it was done.

"Kayla, I sat there for almost three hours and saw just about every cat video, political rant, religious message, and vacation shot that was on Facebook. I drank two Venti

Frappuccinos at a grand total of fourteen dollars. I had work to do so, I walked over to the garage and inquired about my van.

'Oh hey,' smiled Rich in a condescending way. His face said *I'm an asshole*, the jerk. 'Van's done. Hate to tell ya but it needed a whole new set of brakes. Tried to call ya...no answer, so I did it knowin' how much you need it an' all,' he told me while chewing on something, probably his cud.

"You tried to call?" I was holding my phone the whole time I waited! "Wow, they were just grabbing a bit," I replied. I wanted to yell; *Are you so stupid you can't read a phone number?"*

'Yeah, that's a sign they were shot. Good thing you came in when you did.'

This sure didn't sound good to me, but I had to ask.

"So, what's the damage?"

"He picked up his clipboard, grinned widely, and said, 'Two thousand...that's including your oil change.'

"I couldn't believe it. "*What, two thousand for a brake job? You're kidding me.*" No way would your father spend that kind of money on the van.

"Then, he said, 'And an oil change. You see, it's an industrial van. It needed special parts like special brake pads, special rotors, and special calipers. That stuff is expensive.'

"It's a Ford van. Not a special Ford van. It's just a Ford van!" I was exasperated. We stood there staring at each other, when something totally from left field escaped my lips and ran with it. "Would you give me a nice big discount for a good home cooked meal?" I smiled demurely at this butt crack. Obviously, something way back in my mind's recesses had a plan."

'Heck, yeah. I heard you're a good cook.' He leaned in toward me. I could smell his; *I just ate doo doo breath.* Ugh!

"*Six then?*" I asked while trying to maintain the contents of my stomach."

'Oh, I'll be there. I'll just hold onto this bill here until tomorrow...dependin' on how good dinner is,' he winked.'

"The nerve...depending on how good dinner is.

So, I made a lovely Chicken Marsala loaded with some nice mushrooms I found by my Oak tree."

"Aren't they poisonous?" Kayla blinks. She somehow knows what her mother's answer will be.

"I wasn't really sure if they were. They're pretty mushrooms with a light green cap with pure white gills. I fried them in a mixture of butter and garlic, blended in the chicken breasts and finished with lots of Marsala wine and cream. Luscious."

Kayla's mind refuses to comprehend what her mother has become. "Mom, they could have killed you.

Why would you do that?"

"I just thought they would make Rich sick. I didn't eat any. Gosh, I'm not that stupid," Melanie continues, "Anyway, he was right on time wearing a teal Hawaiian shirt. It appeared as though he took a shower. His hair wasn't as greasy, and his hands were mostly clean. It was filthy under his finger-nails--something your father would never tolerate. When he gave me a "hello" peck on the lips, ugh, his breath smelled the same—like chewing on a dirty diaper. He brought a cheap bottle of Merlot which we drank with our meal. He relished dinner, raving about it.

He said I was the best cook in Rockwell. He was almost likable...until after dinner.

"We went to the living room and sat on the couch. I had hoped after he ate so many mushrooms, he'd be too sick to stay and visit. No such luck. He began pawing at me and kissing me. He tried to put his nasty tongue in my mouth. I bit it. It turned him on. He groped at me."

Kayla gasped, "Oh, Mom."

"Good Lord, I worried that I had picked good mushrooms. I had to think of a way to get him off me. I had to buy some time. I excused myself to go to the bathroom and think."

'Whoa, your couch is trying to eat me.' When I came back into the living room, the man was flopping all over the place. He somehow wedged himself between the cushions.

'Help!' he yelled, when all of a sudden, he calmed down and stood up.

"Then I understood what was going on. He was tripping from the mushrooms.

Whew, it's kinda hot in here. Why do you have a fire goin' in the middle of your living room?'

"He was staring at the lamp on my end table. He began to walk toward the kitchen. 'Whoa, you need to fix your floor...it's all wobbly and shit. It's makin' me seasick,' he slurred, careening through the door of the kitchen--his arms and legs flailing about. He was walking like he was seriously drunk.

'Ack, I'm going to hurl,' he said, before spewing all over the kitchen floor. He glanced at me with sad puppy dog eyes. 'I'm sorry, I tried to make it to the toilet.' He pointed at the kitchen sink.

'Man, I don't feel too good. I think it's something I ate. My tummy's crampin' fierce,' he moaned. "He was leaning down to get on all fours.

"I think it was the mushrooms," I panicked.

'Call 911,' he cried.

"No time. I'll take you to the hospital myself," I told him. I hoisted him back to his feet. He leaned on me, and I guided him to the van, and eased him into the passenger seat.

'Hurry.' He was looking bad. His face was turning yellow.

"I started the van and drove...around the block. I thought his reaction to the mushrooms would pass and I would have the satisfaction of getting back at Rich for overcharging me. I couldn't take him to the hospital. They would ask all kinds of questions and charge me with attempted murder or something like that. I thought he had passed out. I tried to shake him awake with no luck. I didn't mean to kill him, so I took him to Tiger

World and parked the van by the woods."

"What? Mom..." Kayla's eyes grow wide. *There IS something wrong with her.* "Mom, you didn't..."

"What else could I do? I fed him those mushrooms. I'm a murderer!" Melanie cried, but no tears welled in her eyes. In fact, there was an up curl of her lips. There was some satisfaction of getting rid of a man who would rip off women in her face.

"You poisoned him because you didn't want to spend the money?"

"No, it was the point. He was ripping me off...and he was gross."

*

The afternoon sun grows hot as Jerry walks. He still has a few miles to go. The shade under a big Live Oak tree is irresistible. He plops onto the soft grass, lifts his soda from the bag, and opens it. The can erupts into a fizzy cola lava flow. Jerry quickly drinks half of it down before any more drips onto his hands. He wipes them on his pants before finishing his drink. He has the odd feeling he's being watched, like when his mother hovers behind him to make sure he gets every dish spotless. Spinning around, Jerry expects to find the panther his father described, but finds a squirrel edging toward him searching for a treat. The swiftness of Jerry's spin causes the critter to run up the tree.

"Sorry...little guy." Jerry stands, stretches, and picks up his sacks to continue on his way.

*

Kayla covers her ears with her hands. Melanie pulls them away. "I drug Rich out of the van and was waiting for Grimalkin to come out when I heard a motorcycle approaching. It stopped nearby. I hid and watched the rider lurk around the cages. He was approaching Rich, so I came out of hiding and asked if I could help him. Of course, I didn't want to. I wanted him out of there. It surprised and threw me off guard when he introduced himself, and said he was a friend of Brian Mumert's. He was looking for him.

"Right away I blurted, "Who would be here...at this hour?" Oh geez, sure that sounded fishy.

'You are,' he said, raising his eyebrows. 'And what happened to him?' He was pointing at Rich.

"Oh, he had a little too much to drink. We were out partying before coming here. He passed out."

'And why are you here?'

"I feed the tigers...isn't it obvious?" I asked opening the back doors of the van. Fresh meat odor wafted into the air. I held up a handful of meat I scooped out of a box.

'So why you feeding them in the middle of the night?'

"The owner prefers it that way because we feed them...uh, horse meat. She doesn't want PETA on her case." It was the perfect answer.

'Hell, I get that. Hey, a horse has to go somewhere, no use wasting it.'

"I nodded, and proceeded to finish feeding them, hoping he would go away, but no such luck.

'He loved tigers,' Skillet continued. 'He would come here late at night just to watch them pace in their pen. He told me they're more alert at night. They made him feel peaceful.'

"I almost laughed. How ironic is that?" Melanie didn't wait for an answer before going on with her story.

'Wait a minute,' his eyes grew wide with recognition. 'You were at the bar the night he disappeared. He guided you to your house!'

"Oh," I acted surprised. "You're looking for that guy? His name was Mumert...that's right. Wow, small world," I said, while thinking of a way to get rid of this guy.

"Oh, gosh," an idea came to me. "You know, he left his wallet at my house, the big one he attaches to his pants with a chain? We got rather frisky that night and he removed it. I never got the chance to return it."

'You just told me you didn't know him,' Skillet accused.

"Well, I didn't really know him. I mean it happened like a month ago." Shoot, this guy was smarter than I thought.

'Where is it? You're in deep shit if you robbed him. Where is he?' he demanded.

"I don't know where he is," I said, glancing over at the woods. I was hoping Grimalkin would leap out and take this guy down. "The wallet's in my van. His money is still in it. I'm not a thief!"

'Give it to me,' he growled louder than the tigers.

"I walked over to the van. 'It's in the back somewhere.' Darn if he didn't go over and check on Rich. He took his pulse.

'Hey, this guy is dead!'

"I...wow, you know, he must have over-dosed. He was taking drugs too. Gosh.

"He stormed toward me, 'You know what happened to Mumert!'

"I do not!" I retorted.

"He glared at me hard. I was almost frightened.

'I'll get to the bottom of this. I think you know where Mumert is. Get his wallet...now!' I was relieved he was falling for my plan.

"I crawled into the back and began rooting around. I didn't have Mumert's wallet. I was trying to stall for time. I got rid of it, and there was only five bucks in it. He was accusing me of murder. It could have been the end of everything. I searched and found a hypodermic needle full of my horse tranquilizer. I prayed it would work. I slowly crawled out, acting like I got the wallet, and saw the big man's thigh near the door. I swung back hard as I could, pushing the needle into his leg and squeezed down on the plunger.

"He went insane with anger. He grabbed me by the leg and swiftly pulled me out of the van cutting my arm on one of my tools."

Kayla searches for a way to escape. Her mother sits her back down. She's performing for a captive audience of one.

'You bitch!' he yelled and punched me in the gut. I reeled backwards, blacking out. He pulled me up onto my feet to face him. 'You better tell me where Mumert is, or you die!'

"Might as well tell a dying man what he wanted to know, so I pointed at the woods. "In there," I whispered. 'What are you talkin' about?' Skillet squinted toward the woods. Grimalkin crept out of them and laid down on the ground glaring at the man. All the activity and violence agitated the tigers. They paced and growled--showing their gleaming teeth.

"In her," I corrected.

"He stood there for a moment. A mixture of surprise and shock spread over his face--his vice grip on me unwavering. Blood trickled down my T-shirt from the gash on my arm. I was hoping Grimalkin would come and eat him right then.

'Why you...' He brought both of his hands to my neck. I tried to deflect him with no luck causing the blood from my wound to spray over his shirt and face. It incited him even more.

"He squeezed my neck like the jerk of a hangman's noose. I instantly couldn't breathe. Visions of my father choking my mother came to my mind. They say your life flashes before you in the moments before death. I saw my father trying to kill my mother. I was hoping for much better. I fell to my knees...so did Skillet. His grip loosened and he became groggy. The Goliath fell over hard. He was down but, he wasn't out. The tigers roared. Grimalkin crept closer. I jumped into my van and locked the door afraid my bleeding arm would attract her. She sniffed at him and licked my blood from his face. Skillet's eyes...I'll never forget the look of sheer horror in them. She opened her huge jaws and clamped down on his head. I couldn't stop watching her. She was a sight of magnificence with her glistening fur, her muscles straining to drag him into her woods...powerful."

Melanie stares into space, remembering the moment.

"Mom," Kayla interrupts. "We need to go now. The police need to know everything. We can't go on like this."

Melanie continues as if she isn't hearing a word Kayla is saying.

"I was so enamored I had forgotten about my arm. I had to get to a hospital. It had bled a great deal and I was feeling weak and woozy. When I walked into the emergency room, I was met with shocked stares. There was a great deal of blood all over me. I must have looked like Stephen King's *Carrie*."

"You told me you accidently cut it leaning on a blade in the shop."

"I wasn't ready to tell you about it then. I told the girl at the desk that I had accidently cut my arm while butchering a pig. She didn't even flinch. I drove home after three hours of waiting and getting ten stitches. I had hoped that Grimalkin would take Rich too, but apparently, she didn't like his taste. I wouldn't either," Melanie chuckles. "I left him there. I didn't know what else I could do at the time."

"Mom, the police will track you down. They'll know it was your fault Rich died," Kayla sobs.

"Only if you tell them. They'll find out Rich had a bad meal of mushrooms. That's not my fault, Kayla. Very bad things will happen if you tell the police otherwise. Don't even think about it."

Kayla puts her face in her hands and sobs. "But they'll question why he was there. It doesn't make sense."

"Promise me," Melanie takes Kayla by the shoulders and gives her a shake to emphasize each word.

"I...I promise, Mommy. Please don't hurt me."

*

"Bout time, I been waitin' for my meds." Jerry's mother is where he left her...Pa's easy chair.

Jerry knows she can get it herself, yet he obediently gives her the bag of cash and runs into the kitchen to fetch her medicine. She pushes herself from the chair holding the bag. "And where's my damn cottage cheese?"

"Come...coming." Jerry scoops cottage cheese into a bowl at the same time pulling open the silverware drawer.

Ma squinches her eyes, drawing her mouth downward in her best effort, which isn't hard, to appear stupid. She mimics Jerry. "Come, I said...come...coming. Retard," she mumbles.

Jerry rushes into the living room holding the bowl of cheese and meds. Ma is hiding cash under sofa cushions, under the easy chair and behind the TV. He doesn't understand why she stashes it instead of using it.

"Ma...why don't...we...we go...away?"

Ignoring him, she continues to hide money. She opens a door on the side table and places cash on a huge stack inside.

He places her bowl of cottage cheese on the coffee table to gaze at a framed photo on the fireplace mantel.

It's the only photo Jerry knows of in the house. It's of his parents on the beach. They're young and smiling. Each has an arm around the other. Ma used to tell him stories about the beach and how much fun she and Pa had together there. He picks up the frame. "We...can go...to the beach...now."

Ma swoops on him tearing the photo from his hands and slamming it face down back on the mantel. "It's too late...look at me!" She grabs her son's head in her hands and forces his head up to look her in the eyes.

Jerry blinks. He hadn't realized this is a much older woman than the one in the photograph. The lines in her face, the droop of her eyes, the gray in her hair makes him realize she is much older now in spirit since Pa died. Her gnarled arthritic hands releases his face.

"I'm not goin' anywhere. My legs kill me walkin' to the damn bathroom. I sure as Hell can't walk on the beach." She eases herself into Pa's chair and swings her arm toward the bowl. "Gimme that."

Jerry hands her the cottage cheese. Ma's cheeks are moist from tears leaking from her eyes. He knows better than to say anything about it.

*

"Oh my..." Melanie takes her daughter in her arms and holds her. "I could never hurt you. You are the only good that has ever happened in my life. It's all been in self-defense."

Melanie pauses to think. She chuckles, "Remember Bill? Our bible thumping Republican neighbor who hasn't been to church for years? And he was a peeping Tom."

"He was?" Kayla pulls up the edge of her shirt to wipe at her tears.

"Definitely a bad man. He couldn't peek through our windows since we have light blocking curtains over them, but many times I'd spotted him in other neighbors' yards at their windows craning his neck for a good look. Disgusting.

"He lived alone after his wife left him six years ago. They had been married for twenty-five. I guess it took her that long to catch him doing it.

"In the past, your father had been giving him cuts of meat to keep him from complaining about our noise. I think he wanted to complain because he couldn't see what we were doing. Sure enough, while I was at my van preparing to make deliveries, the man appeared out of nowhere.

'Hello, Mrs. Williams,' he called out to me cheerfully.

"I nodded to him, "Hello, Bill."

'Not to bother you or anything, but...'

"Oh, he bothers me, all right. Of course, he went on.

'I haven't seen your mister for a while. Hope everything is okay,' he continued.

"Everything is fine," I said. "He had to leave town to care for his sick father."

'Oh? Well, I'll certainly be saying a prayer for him and his family, God bless.'

"What a hypocrite, "Thank you...well, it's been...I need to get to my deliveries. You have a ..." I was trying to think of a way to get away from him. I opened the door to the van.

'I sure miss that meat your husband sends my way. Sure would be a shame, at this time of family crisis, to have to close your shop for breaking the noise ordinance and all. I'm sure you understand,' he smiled a wide greedy smile...the leech. I understood all right.

"I could feel my lips tug at the corners of my mouth sensing it was more of a grimace than a smile. I slammed the van door shut. "Of course, you know, I think Rob left a special cut just for you."

'I thought so,' he beamed as he rubbed his hands together.

"I opened the shop door and let him in. He gazed around the workshop.

'Holy moley,' he exclaimed. 'This is a real professional operation.'

"Of course, it is. We serve only the best to the tigers at the zoo...and indeed, to you," I forced myself to smile. I opened the door to the walk-in freezer. "Your cuts are in there, I'll be with you in a minute," I said. He entered the walk-in freezer. I wanted to shut him inside. He disgusted me, but Kayla, I'm not a killer. I didn't do that. I just went and got the dolly to pick up a box of meat for him.

'Oh, my dear God,' I could hear real fear in his voice. It gave me goosebumps. I walked in and saw him gazing at the horse hanging in the freezer. 'I didn't know you butcher horses. Is that in my meat?' he asked.

"No," I assured him. "It's only grade A for you."

'What a relief. Where is its head?'

"We send heads to fertilizer plants."

'Animal heads are in my fertilizer?' he asked aghast.

"Most probably. What? You want them in landfills wasting our natural resources? They're being returned to the earth. It's a beautiful thing. When I die, I want to be turned into fertilizer," I told him.

'That's disgusting. Where's my meat? I don't want to see this anymore,' he said practically jogging out of there.

I put the dolly under a box and rolled it out to him.

"You can use this to get your meat home. I would appreciate it if you would bring it right back."

"He leaned down to pick up the box. 'I got it. I can pick up a box of meat.' He strained lifting it, lost his balance, and fell over my lift...backwards. His head hit the cement. He was gone, just like that.

"You called an ambulance, right? I mean, that was a real accident," Kayla feels the lump returning to her throat knowing it was a useless question.

"No. Are you serious? Kayla this is the real world. That ugly man, by falling down, would have caused the end of my business. They would've investigated permits, safety, licenses...all of it. We have none of it. Your father hated bureaucracy. The farms who donated the meat and the animals we bought never asked for things like permits. I must keep our business going...I don't know how to do anything else. I'm in charge—I have nobody to answer to.

"Where is he? What...what did you do with him," Kayla asks her bottom lip quivering.

Melanie nods toward the walk-in freezer. "He's in there."

"If detective Billings comes back, he'll find him in there," tears are running down Kayla's cheeks.

"True, maybe...but not the way he looks now. I prepared him like I do meat. He actually looks like a side of beef," Melanie smiles. "Do you want to see him?"

"No!" Kayla cowers away from her mother. "His...head...?"

"I buried it in the back yard."

Kayla swallows back the contents of her stomach burning up her throat.

"Look, I had to," Melanie shrugs. "At first, I drug him out the back door in hopes Grimalkin would take him away. I even called for her. She never came, so I did the only thing I knew how to do—besides, there wasn't any more room in the chest freezer."

Kayla's whole being slumps. "Dad..."

"Yes, your dad. I was thinking about butchering him, I mean meat...is meat. I don't think Grimalkin will eat him in this state. He's too tough and leathery by now," Melanie says frankly.

"Mom! Seriously. What are you saying? Something is wrong with you,"

"Don't you talk to me like that, little girl. Things just happened. I'm fine, and you'll be fine too once this is all over. We can keep your father in the freezer for the time being. We'll just cover him up again and pray detective Billings never comes back. Okay dokey?"

Kayla nods slowly and wonders how this mess will ever be *all over.*

Melanie stands and straightens herself. "I'm so relieved you know everything. I hate secrets. Now, we have another issue we must address. I went out last night to Tiger World and an old F-150 truck was there. I snuck up to the cabin of the truck. No one was in it. I saw a gun rack on the rear window with two rifles in it. The driver's side door was hanging open. It looked like it had been ripped open. I saw claw marks on it. I looked inside and saw a huge puddle of blood on the seat. I knew then they were hunters after Grimalkin and she took care of the problem, just the way I dispersed of mine," Melanie smiles wide, proud of what the beast did.

"I decided to get rid of any evidence. If the police have found it, they would have hunted her down and killed her. They need to be searching for a murderer, I have to protect her. The keys were still in the truck. So, I found a tarp in the back, draped it over the driver's seat and drove it to the back of the old tire store across the street. There is so much junk behind that shop no-one will ever notice. Lea, the owner of Tiger World, gave me a ride back to the zoo to retrieve the van. I told her it had run out of gas, so the sweetheart came with a gas can. I was relieved the zoo was closed that day."

"Mom, that's the animal that hurt Nicky."

"I guess it means she can sense bad men."

Melanie smirks. She claps her hands together. "Now, you and I need to go to Tiger World to get rid of traps I found there before Grimalkin gets hurt."

"Traps?"

"Yes, bear traps of all things. They're lining the woods. Now, I understand why Grimalkin didn't come for her dinner. I need help cleaning them up."

"What about Grimalkin?"

"She won't bother us. She'll know we're helping her."

Kayla shivers all down her spine.

"Mom, Nick is not bad. I haven't heard from him. He isn't in there, is he?" Kayla points toward the walkin freezer.

There is no response from her mother.

"Not Nick, God, no!" Kayla screams as she runs toward the freezer. *It all has to be the most horrible nightmare of my life.*

Kayla pulls open the door to a sight worse than any of her nightmares, worse than any horror film she has seen...worse than any of her scary stories. Hanging on huge metal hooks suspended from the ceiling of the walk-in freezer is a headless human torso and a horse. They are stripped of skin showing veins of dark meat, muscle, and sinew. Her breath leaves her.

Kayla blacks out again. When she comes to, the "meat" is still there. She spits bile after throwing up everything else in her stomach. Melanie is at her side with a cool damp rag placed on her head.

"I know it's hard to take all of this in. It was for me too at first," her mother soothes. "As you can see poor Nick is not in there."

"You fed him to the panther?" Kayla screams.

"Tsk, no, silly. I'm not the evil witch of the west. I don't approve of Nick, but I'm not going to kill him.

Gosh no...unless he tries to hurt you—then, it's game on. I'm just saying."

"He's okay?"

"As far as I know."

"Mom, this is a small town. They're hunting Grimalkin. You're using her to get away with murder."

"It was never murder! It was self-defense. I told you that!"

It is all so surreal. "Mom..."

"You know what? Grimalkin and I are doing you...and the world, a huge favor by eliminating them."

Her mother stands tall, full of pride. "I actually performed a public service. I'm ridding the world of vermin and caring for the animals at the zoos and the last panther in North Carolina. Tiger World wouldn't be in operation without me...*and* I'm keeping Grimalkin healthy."

"What?"

"I feed her. I think she likes me," Melanie smiles in an insane odd way.

"But Mom...this...this is all wrong. It's wrong," Kayla sobs.

"You tell me how...huh? Our lives are going to be so much better. Grimalkin and I rid our lives of bad men. We're making better money than ever. Grimalkin came right when I needed her. She's the only one of her kind...and so am I."

Kayla stands and numbly walks over to the freezer where her father lies. "I guess you can say he was a bad man. He hurt you, but I know he loved us. He had a bad temper that he couldn't control. He was under a lot of pressure, like you. He needed help...not killed." Kayla gazes upon her father's glazed frozen eyes.

"His death was an accident. I just didn't call an ambulance. He was going to kill me. Kayla, I'm not a murderer." Her mother spins Kayla around to face her, palms in prayer.

"Maybe we can give him a nice burial when this is all over." Kayla slowly turns back and closes the lid of the freezer.

"Oh, dear," Melanie tsks. "Why don't you have some milk and go to bed now. You need the rest after all of this," she smiles sweetly.

Kayla stumbles away, into her bedroom and grabs her phone. She dials Uncle Mike. *He'll help me stop this.* His phone rings several times. Her heart thumps heavily in her neck. She's shaking. *Please answer your phone!*

"Hello?" Relief.

"Uncle Mike!"

"Hey, K K," *he sounds so normal.* Kayla glances up. Melanie is pointing a gun at her. "Hello? Hello?"

"Give it to me," Her mother whispers harshly. Kayla obeys and hands her the phone.

"Mike." Cheer in her voice as though nothing is going on. "Oh, Kayla's just being a bit unruly. I need help in the shop, and she'd rather go to your house to escape it."

She pauses, listening. "No, I fired him. He was mean to the tigers and scared Kayla. It's just too hard to trust another one after that," she hesitates again.

"Believe me I give her plenty of free time. Listen, I'd love to chat, but like I said, we're really busy right now. Give Sheila and the baby my love. Okay? Love you too...bye."

Melanie drops Kayla's phone and stomps on it. The screen shatters, the battery falls out. Pieces are scattered about. She scoops up the battery and pockets it.

"You would shoot me?" Kayla screams.

"I will do whatever it takes. No one is going to take me down. I mean no one!"

She is talking to ME...her daughter. Something has gone terribly wrong.

Melanie nods toward the kitchen. "Get your drink and go to bed. We have a lot to do in the morning." Kayla cries drinking her milk. She doesn't know what to do. When she finishes, her tears are gone. All that is left is a milky film in the glass...and over her eyes.

Kayla's phone is a total loss. She lost her mother too...somewhere between the death of her father and one of the "bad men" who have died because of her. Grimalkin could be stalking Nick and now that her phone is dead, she fears she will never know. She drifts into a fitful sleep.

A revving car engine wakes her. Kayla runs to her window. Melanie is pulling out of the drive in the van. There is something else. A huge shadow lopes across the street toward the tire shop. *It could be Grimalkin!* She has an undeniable urge to see it.

The tire shop is closed. All that illuminates it is a lone streetlight. She grabs a flashlight and runs across the street hoping nobody sees her. Kayla shines her light through the glass in the front door. Tires and equipment are scattered about inside, but no sign of Grimalkin.

Kayla builds up the courage lurk around to the back. It's dark and eerie. The light of the moon casts shadows on the junk and bushes making them all appear as hunched over creatures.

She gets up her nerve and edges around the corner. An old Ford F-150 truck is centered in the glow of her flashlight beam...and so is a pair of glowing yellow eyes staring right at her from above the steering wheel. Kayla stiffens and doesn't move a muscle, and neither do those eyes...glaring back at her unblinking. The driver's door is open. She holds her light onto those eyes while slowly backing up. Suddenly, they move toward the door.

Kayla screams and runs home locking the door behind her. She peeks out the front window. A neighbor's porch light comes on. She considers running over for help when a raccoon plods from behind the tire shop into the glow of the streetlight. The neighbors turn off their light, and

Kayla takes a deep breath of relief. She prays her mother didn't leave to go murder Nick by accident. She can't sleep. It is all too much.

*

Jerry gazes at the ceiling from his bed. He can't go to sleep. He thinks about his mother's unhappiness. He has rarely seen her smile. She probably wouldn't look so old if she smiled more, but he doesn't seem to bring her joy, never did. He wasn't born the perfect child she imagined, besides, she thought she was too old to have children. Jerry was an unhappy surprise that she kept hidden from the world until he became too old, and even then, his parents told folks he was a slow cousin they allowed to live with them. He closes his eyes, air slipping from his lungs. He wants to see more of the world than his town. He wants to see what made his parents so happy. He wants to go to the beach.

Chapter 11

A Discovery

Mike can't sleep. He thinks about how strange Kayla and Melanie seemed on the phone. Kayla sounded like she was in a panic and that was the fakest cheery tone he has ever heard from Melanie. Maybe Rob came back and he's threatening the girls. Mike wants to drop everything and run over there--but if he's not smart, he could become a victim himself. He needs to find out what is going on. Mumert has disappeared, and now, so has Skillet. Maybe they came across the panther? Mike feels he owes it to them to find out. *Who knows? Maybe they're still alive?*

Noah is nine weeks old already and Sheila is doing just fine. She has a few weeks left before going back to work. Mike convinces her to spend some time with Noah at her mother's in Charlotte. It gives her a little vacation away from any chance they could be in danger. It's one less thing for Mike to worry about.

Mike plans his search. He gasses up the car and takes Shep along with him. The dog has a great nose, and he can protect Mike if there's any trouble. He makes a great partner. The Uwharrie Forest is near Buddy's Tavern where Mumert and Skillet hung out. Mike decides to begin a search there.

Mike and Shep head out in the morning. He's heard of weird stuff happening in forests—like satanic rituals with human sacrifice, Big Foot, bears, and aliens. This morning, before heading out, Mike watched an interview with a hillbilly in a dirty undershirt tell the newsman that the creature killing folks isn't a panther...it's Bog Woman. The guy even held up a photo. It looked like a Sasquatch. He said Bog Woman is keeping the guys in the forest somewhere for mating purposes.

Dumbass, Mike chuckles to himself. Shep gazes up at him and wags his tail. "Shep, watch out for Bog

Women. I don't want to get molested by some hairy beast...course now, if she has a nice..." Shep barks, interrupting his comment.

Mike parks his car at the head of a hiking trail. Shep goes nuts--barking and pacing and scratching to get out of the car. It's all Mike can do to get the leash on him. Shep pulls hard on it leading Mike down a path. About a half mile in, he veers from it. His bark turns to a frantic high pitch yanking Mike through brush and thorns. They run into a clearing. Shep ambles toward a mound covered with leaves from the forest floor. He begins digging frantically whisking leaves and dirt from the spot. Mike can tell that it's freshly dug earth. He sees a flash of white in the ground where Shep is digging, then hair.

The dog begins to whine. Mike runs to Shep and brushes more dirt away. It's Mumert! Shep and Mike dig dirt away from him. Shep immediately moves to lick him and stops in mid-lick. He sniffs at his old buddy and winces back. Mumert has been dead for a while, and it shows in his face. His skin is pure white and puffy, eyes totally sunken into his head. His cheeks are moving almost like he is chewing on something. The smell is putrid. Shep cocks his head one way, then another. He keens, suffering from terrible pain.

Mike finds a stick and pokes at one cheek. It pops like a huge boil. Puss doesn't emerge from it--thousands of maggots do. Mike gags turning away from it until he gains composure. Shep is digging again. In terror, Mike sees what he is digging up. It's another body! This one isn't gone as long; it has puncture marks. Mike spreads his fingers over the man's face. The marks align with his fingers giving him chills. It's Skillet. Mike shakes himself to his senses. With a racing heart, he stands glancing about praying he isn't being watched or followed. Shep continues his baleful howl. Mike pets

Shep in an attempt to soothe him. They are both a mess. "Melanie and Kayla are in danger," Mike says aloud to Shep. "This could be Rob's doing, or that creature, or God knows...maybe a cult. I've got to get to them. I could never live with myself if I let something happen to them."

Shep yips in agreement.

He tries to call detective Billings, but there is little cell phone reception in the forest. Shep and Mike run to his car.

*

When Kayla walks into the kitchen early the next morning, she gives her mother an angry glare. Melanie has never seen Kayla look at her like that before. She wants to smack that look off of her daughter's face, but it would lower her to the likes of Rob.

"You didn't kill Nicky, did you?" Kayla asks.

"I told you, of course not," Her mother answers.

"You're not planning to kill him, are you?"

"No harm will come to him…as long as he leaves you alone. You two were getting too chummy. You're only fourteen. He's two years older than you. You need to find someone your own age."

"Mom!"

Melanie pauses to place her hand on her daughter's sweet head. Kayla shoves it away. It hurt.

"I went ahead and cleared out the traps. They're hard to see at night. I didn't want Grimalkin to get hurt on one of those things, and you were sleeping so sound, I didn't want to disturb you. You've been through enough. Kayla, my sweet girl, you must know about men like Nick. All they want is someone to wait on them hand and foot and cook for them. They want to be their woman's whole life. They aren't worth the trouble."

"Mom! We're just friends. I can't believe you," Kayla cries. She runs into her room and slams the door.

Melanie follows. "Right, I know better. Boys full of testosterone can't be just friends." She pounds on the door. "Kayla, come out right this minute. We have work to do."

No answer.

"Now! Don't make me do the unthinkable."

Melanie really doesn't know what unthinkable thing she is talking about. She had to say whatever it will take to get Kayla out of her room to help her. Melanie stomps down the hall loudly into the kitchen. Kayla sheepishly comes out of her room and joins her mother.

"If I promise to stay away from him, will you promise not to kill him? Please?"

Melanie smiles warmly at her sweet child, "I promise, now let's eat breakfast and get to work."

After breakfast they go to the shop and suit up in aprons and gloves. There is meat to process in the van. Melanie rolls it onto a forklift. Then, Kayla drives the meat into the walk-in freezer and her mother hoists it onto a hook. When they are in the freezer, they must keep the door open. Rob had removed the interior door handle as a threat to put Melanie in it for punishment. She's relieved he didn't live long enough to follow through on that threat and reminds herself to get it fixed. She'll feel horrible if Kayla ever gets accidently stuck inside.

"Should we process him?" Melanie nods toward Bill hanging in the walk-in freezer.

"No!" Kayla sucks in cold air to calm herself.

"Could you do it when I'm not around...please?"

"Sure thing," Melanie smiles. She continues on her work humming the tune, *You Are My Sunshine.*

Kayla buries her face in her hands.

"Come along, we got to get this done," Melanie drives the fork-lift into the walk-in freezer to retrieve the side of beef.

Kayla creeps toward the door. She pauses with her hand on it. Seconds feel like minutes. *I should close this door. She needs to be stopped...but she's the only mother I've known.*

Her mother hums happily as she works. "We got a lot done, honey. We're almost finished for today and I'm starving...how about you?" Melanie is cheerful driving out of the freezer with the beef. She offers to treat Kayla to dinner. Kayla doesn't want to go. Her stomach churns with the thought but nods her head in agreement.

Chapter 12

Confrontations

Mike runs to his car and finds he finally has reception. In a panic, he taps *camera* instead of the phone icon. When he finally taps *phone*, he doesn't see detective Billings' number, just the dial screen. Seconds count. He taps *recent* and locates the detective's number. Mike taps on it and waits for a ring tone...nothing. He looks down at his phone to discover he must hit the green *phone* icon before it will dial. *I knew that!* He tells himself to calm down, yet his hands are shaking uncontrollably.

Shep leans on him as if to say, *pet me, that will help.* Mike pets him. The throbbing in his throat slows down. He begins to collect his wits when Shep utters a low growl. Mike glances up from his phone. There is movement in the brush. He instinctively grabs the dog's leash while holding his phone. Shep lunges—Mike's phone flies out of his hand.

Something...or someone is in the brush. Shep strains against his leash, howling and snapping. It takes all of Mike's strength to hold him back while searching for the phone. Mike wishes he had a gun on him.

A huge black shape emerges from the cover of the forest. A bear--and it's heading straight for Shep. Mike dives into the back seat of the car pulling on the leash. Shep is completely focused on the bear, his muzzle pulled back showing his chops, fur standing straight up on his neck. The bear rises up on its hind haunches and roars. Mike jerks Shep with all of his might into the car. He slams the door shut. The bear presses its face against the window. It claws at the door and pounds on the car, rocking it with every pounce. Shep snarls and snaps at the window. Finally, after several harrowing minutes, the bear shambles away, followed by two cubs. Shep gives her a farewell bark.

Mike eases out of the car looking for his phone and finds it on the gravel drive of the parking area. The screen is shattered. He tries to turn it on...nothing.

Damn! Mike tosses the phone into his pocket and runs back to the car. He must get to Melanie's.

*

Melanie claps her hands together, "Job well done. Now, let's go to dinner." She says it like it is a lovely sunny day and they're going on a picnic.

"Afterwards, I'll take you to Tiger World to feed the tigers and Grimalkin. You'll see how gorgeous she is, and we'll check for traps."

She takes Kayla to the Red Lobster near Charlotte.

Kayla's stomach turns considering the lobsters with their claws held shut with a rubber band. They're helpless. Anything could grab them and eat them without a worry. The lobsters have no defense. You could say their hands are tied. Kayla imagines the men who died were like lobsters in a tank. If those lobsters were to be set free, something else will eat them...a big fish, parasites, bugs, and worms. Everything eats everything.

She loses her appetite. Melanie orders fried shrimp for Kayla while she has the lobster. Kayla picks at her food and wonders about how shrimp swim while her mother rambles on about how they're making more money than her father ever did and they'll move into a nicer home maybe in the city, and they'll go on nice vacations like Disney World, and blah, blah, blah. Kayla hates Disney World. *It's too...cute!*

Melanie cracks open a lobster claw digging out the meat. She dips it in butter. "Maybe we will move somewhere beautiful, like Belize, or Grand Cayman

Island. Wouldn't that be awesome?" The buttered white claw guts enter her mother's mouth. She chews with relish.

A volcano of anger erupts from Kayla. "No! I want to live near Uncle Mike. I want to babysit little Noah, and I have friends there, and I want to go to school there." She is sure her real mother wouldn't act the way this woman is behaving.

"Uh, huh...the "friend" you refer to is Nick. You might as well forget about him."

"Thanks to you!" Kayla shoots back. "Mom, I don't know you anymore. I think Aliens took over your body. My real mom would have trusted me. She would have believed me. She wouldn't be...mur...doing this!"

"Shhh, you're over-reacting." Melanie leans over her dish toward Kayla whispering harshly. "I just don't want you to make the same mistakes that I have. I went for the first boy that showed any interest in me."

"I'm not you, Mom, and..." a huge lump forms in Kayla's throat making it nearly impossible to speak without crying. "I want my old Mom back. I want Mommy."

Melanie takes Kayla in her arms and rocks her, like her mother again...for a minute. "Don't you see? I'm the new and improved Mommy. I'm independent Mom. I can run a business by myself. I feed our lovely, endangered animals, and I don't have to worry about any man dictating who I am," Melanie smiles wide. There's a wild gleam in her eyes. "Now, let's go to the zoo."

When Kayla and Melanie arrive at the tiger's enclosure the animals are antsy—pacing and roaring. Melanie removes a box of meat from the van and tosses it to them. They gobble it up quickly.

She stops. "Listen."

Melanie and Kayla stand still. They hear a cry like a baby in distress. "It's Grimalkin, come on," Melanie orders. They run into the woods toward the sound. Grimalkin's leg is caught in a large foothold trap.

She growls at the girls' approach. Kayla is overwhelmed by the enormity of the beast. It's larger than the tigers.

"We got to get her out before the hunters come to retrieve her." Melanie is winded.

"How? She'll kill one of us!"

"Calm down. Take a deep breath. Your panic will only aggravate her. Just do what I say," Melanie takes off her jacket. She tosses it at Grimalkin's head covering its eyes. The panther immediately calms down. She points at the spring lever attached to the trap. "Step down on this, it'll release the jaws." Kayla stands, shaking.

"Now...hurry."

Kayla steps forward. Grimalkin has leaned as far away from the trap that she can, her front leg caught firmly in the trap's maw. Kayla gingerly places her foot on the lever. Melanie is kneeling on one knee holding the trap still with one hand and pushing on the lever on the opposite side with her other.

"Push down."

Kayla places her weight on the lever releasing the jaws of the trap. Melanie pulls them open. Grimalkin is still. Melanie silently stands and pulls the jacket off of

Grimalkin's face. The panther leaps. Melanie falls. Kayla screams. Grimalkin jumps over her and runs into the woods. Melanie quickly gets to her feet and removes the trap.

"Let's go," She demands.

Kayla's legs shake like she's standing in a big bowl of Jello. She wills her legs to run back to the van.

Everything around the zoo falls silent. The tigers huddle into a corner of their cage. Kayla's heart hammers in her chest. She feels an urge to pee. She and her mother stand silent as Grimalkin limps out of the woods. It steals toward Melanie and lies down only feet away from her. Kayla holds her breath. The beast flicks her fluffy tail gazing at her with spooky yellow eyes. Melanie slowly reaches into the window of her van and pulls out a gun.

"Pet her," Melanie orders Kayla.

Kayla doesn't move---her breathing shallow.

Grimalkin emits a rumbling sound...like purring.

"Go ahead; pet her like you did the tigers. You weren't afraid then." Her mother's smile reminds Kayla of the witch who convinced Snow White to eat the apple. Kayla inches forward. She doesn't want to, but something propels her...curiosity? She reaches out to touch the beast. Grimalkin's haunches rise, her hackles up, opening her jaws wide. Huge, sharp white teeth surround Kayla's face.

BANG! Melanie shoots toward the beast—not to hurt her, but to scare her away. Grimalkin scats leaving Kayla unharmed.

"Sorry, I thought she'd let you pet her," Melanie says casually.

Kayla's world is spinning. Black spots interfere with her sight. She forces herself to breathe. A high-pitched scream pierces the air. The tigers roar.

"We better get out of here. The noise is going to attract hunters or the police." Melanie hurries to the van.

Kayla wishes she could run away like Grimalkin just did.

Chapter 13

Trapped

When Mike arrives at Melanie's the van is gone, the shop silent. He and Shep walk to the back of the property. A smoker is there. Next to it is a tarp covering a wood pile. Shep approaches it and paws at it. Mike pulls back the tarp to reveal a motorcycle...Mumert's motorcycle. *What does this all mean?* Mike's head swims in a sea of sticky rice. He sits down on the ground to get his bearings. Shep settles next to him.

Melanie must know about it. He wonders if his sister is capable of doing this. *Maybe Rob made her help him kill the men and leave them in the woods...but what about the teeth marks?* Mike shivers at the thought. *What if Melanie and Kayla are trapped inside? Mike could be killing them...or maybe the panther has hurt them.*

Mike tries the door of the shop. It's locked. He bangs on the door. "Hello? Anyone?" He looks under the mat...no key; under rocks...no luck. He runs his fingers along the door frame and finds it. The key is wedged into the top corner of the frame. Entering the shop, Mike scans the room. Nothing seems out of the ordinary. The room is spotless. The way Rob likes it. Shep lopes calmly into the room which tells Mike nobody else is in there. He approaches the walk-in freezer and opens the door. He turns on the light. Hanging on a hook is the torso of a horse. There is something else hanging behind it. Standing in the doorway, Mike can't quite make out what it is. Whatever mammal it was has been skinned.

He must get a closer look. Shep doesn't want anything to do with it and sits himself by the shop's door.

As Mike approaches the shape, the walk-in door closes behind him. He is more concerned with what is before him, frozen solid, the torso of a man. He has been dressed like an animal with no arms, legs, or head. Mike swallows back chum that is rushing up from his stomach burning his throat. Breathing is difficult. He can't tell who it is.

"This is all worse than I ever imagined," he calls out to Shep.

He rushes to the door to leave. He can't find a handle. He can't pry the door open. Shep is scratching and whining on the other side. *It's freezing in here.*

Damn, I shouldn't have let the door shut. I should have wedged something in it first. Who has a walk-in freezer without an inside handle anyway? He bangs on the door and yells for help.

Silence...except for a distant whine from Shep.

Mike tucks his arms into his T-shirt and hunkers into a ball to stay as warm as possible. After close to an hour he hears a noise...a door. Shep growls and barks like he's going to rip the throat out of whoever made the sound.

Mike bangs on the door. "Help! Help!"

He listens to Melanie yell over Shep's barking.

"Mike, is that you?"

"Yes, please get me out of here. I'm freezing my ass off."

"You broke into the workshop!"

"I didn't break in; I found the key." Silence.

"Mel...What's going on?"

"Uncle Mike!" Kayla's sweet voice.

"Kayla, let me out of here." Footsteps toward the door only to stop suddenly. Muttering. Shep barks again.

"Please...someone," Mike pleads.

Silence for what seems an eternity, then the sound of a deadbolt rod locking into its sleeve.

"Uncle Mike," Kayla is crying. "I can't let you out. You know about them. Mom won't let me help you."

"What?" He can't believe what he's hearing.

"Melanie...I'm your brother. You don't want to do this. It's Rob isn't it? Rob! Rob! Listen, I promise I won't say anything to anyone. Just let me go home to my wife and baby."

"He's dead!" Kayla sobs.

Mike's mind attempts to wrap around what is happening. Footsteps are quickly moving from the door. He must break a promise.

"Kayla...Kayla, stop. I'm your father," he bellows at the top of his lungs.

The footsteps stop.

"Melanie and Rob adopted you for me.

My...girlfriend gave you up and I...I was too young to take care of you."

Muttering...crying.

"K K... I love you."

"Shut up! I'm her mother. You have no right. He's lying sweetheart, don't believe one word he says," Melanie shouts, then silence. Cold, empty silence.

Mike leans against the door praying he will hear the bolt slide out of its sleeve and the door open. Instead, Shep growls. The footfalls fade away and a door slams.

"Shep? Shep are you there?" Shep needs to be there so he wouldn't be alone. The dog whines and scratches at the freezer door. "Good boy. Come on, Shep, you can do it. Open the door, boy. Come on."

As Shep works at the door, Mike realizes he has his phone. He pulls it from his pocket, tries to turn it on, and taps on the broken screen. Dead. He wants to throw it but thinks better of it.

Mike must stay positive despite his situation. *Surely Mel won't let me die here. She's punishing me for finding out the truth...that she's gone psycho. Kayla will talk her into letting me go. At least give me some food.*

He's sure it's only a matter of time before detective Billings gets there. Someone will come across those bodies in the woods and call the police.

*

Mike doesn't know how long he's been waiting. It seems like hours. Shep is silent after giving up on the door. He prays he's still out there. *Melanie wouldn't kill a dog, would she?*

Mike's muscles are becoming stiff. He can't feel the tips of his fingers...so cold. He gazes around the room to find anything that will help him. He nods over at the man's torso. *Is this guy Rob? Naw. This guy is bigger. I wonder what he did to get in this situation.*

"I have had a day from Hell," Mike addresses the cadaver. "So, what are you in here for? Or are you just hanging around?"

*

Kayla can't believe her own mother will kill another human being let alone her own brother. When she tried to let Uncle Mike out of the freezer, her mother said, *you know I will not tolerate disobedience*, and she reached into her purse for her gun.

Kayla sobbed when she pushed the bar into place sealing her Uncle Mike's fate. Shep gazed at her with innocent eyes, confused why his master won't come out of the freezer. When her Uncle Mike yelled, *I'm your father,* her mother screamed at him and said he was lying--*but what if he isn't?* "He's a man, Kayla," she told her. "They say anything to get their way. Leave him. Nobody is going to stop my success." She gave Kayla a suffocating hug, "Nobody," and pushed her out of the shop, locked the door and pocketed the key.

Melanie follows Kayla to her room. "We're doing what we have to do. It's him or us. They'll throw us into prison Kayla. We would die there. This is for our very own survival."

Kayla slams her door in her mother's face. "Shut up, shut uuuuup!" She throws herself on her bed and bawls. *Our lives will never be the same again. Little Noah will grow up without his Daddy. I won't even get to see Noah when we move to another country. First, she puts Dad in the freezer, then three more guys die because of her, she butchers another one and hangs him in the freezer, and now, she's killing her own brother and possibly my real father. I don't think he's lying to me. I could have had a real family, a real little brother, and real friends. I'll never know for sure because she's killing him, and if I try to stop her, she'll kill me too. I know it. I've lost my mother.* Kayla buries her face into her pillow and cries until it is soaked. Her face swollen, eyes mere slits, exhaustion takes over her and she falls into fitful sleep.

*

"Damn, it's really cold in here." Mike is shivering uncontrollably. He remembers something he saw Bear Grylls do once on his TV survivor show. He started a fire with a cell phone battery. He doesn't have anything to maintain a fire, but at least he can get it hot enough to warm his hands.

Mike removes the battery from his cell phone. It's very thin--about two and a half inches square. He remembers Bear said to remove the terminal end from it. Mike pushes a bare hook against the terminal. It comes off and he jams the hook into the battery.

Immediately, Mike feels heat emanating from it. He tries to wrap his hands around it. Not only is it too hot to hold onto it begins to sizzle and smoke as lithium meets oxygen. Flames shoot out and he drops it. He rushes toward the heat. It lasts seconds, and now a smoky hot battery stench fills the air in the freezer. Mike coughs to get the dry acidy taste out of his mouth. He needs water.

Mike calls out; his parched throat preventing him from having any real volume in his voice. He's answered with silence. Not even Shep is responding to his calls.

Mike can't stop shivering. He tries to warm part of the horse carcass with his hands to get any kind of fluid from it. It's frozen solid. All it does is make his hands numb. He tries to suck on it, making his throat burn. *God, let me survive the night.*

Chapter 14

Dreams and Nightmares

Melanie can't sleep. She worries she has exposed too much to Kayla too soon. It's been hard for her daughter to adjust to this new life. She even talked back. Her little girl was never like that. Kayla hardly ate any dinner, and she is surly. Melanie needs her cooperation...most of all, she needs Kayla's love. *Mike tried to turn her against me. It won't work. I am her mother. I have been through too much to lose her now.*

For most of her life Melanie's been living in Hell. Kayla is her light through it all. No one should suffer the abuse Melanie survived. She dealt with it every day. It became a normal occurrence. She thought she was smart for leaving home soon as she could, and what does she do? The same thing her mother did. Melanie thought her mother was stupid for staying with that monster; for marrying him in the first place. *I was the stupid one. I shouldn't have left my mother.*

Melanie remembers once jumping on her father's back to make him stop whipping Mike with a belt because he ate the last slice of bologna that their father wanted. He was killing him, so Melanie jumped on his back and hit him in the head. He reeled around, grabbed her by the neck, and pulled her off. Her father wailed on her with his belt. He beat her face, her rear, her legs, arms, and torso. Blood oozed from her nose and around her lips. No one tried to stop him. Melanie's face was swollen, her body bruised. She hurt everywhere. She was angry at her mother for not stopping him and taking her to the hospital. She was in awful pain for days.

Melanie is grateful Mike didn't turn out to be even one bit like their father. He ran away from home right after she left and lived with Mumert's family. Mike made one mistake that became Melanie's blessing. His girlfriend had a baby. She broke up with Mike, gave up

Kayla for adoption and moved to California. He didn't want Kayla to go to a strange family, but he couldn't take care of her. She and Rob took her in. Kayla became their daughter, heart, and soul. Mike promised Melanie he would never tell Kayla she's his daughter. Melanie loves her brother. He has a great job, is married to a wonderful woman, owns a nice home, and has little Noah. He is very dear to her, but he shouldn't have broken that promise. She isn't going to let him take her little girl away.

Kayla eased her loneliness. She's the one smart thing Melanie has ever done. She will die if Kayla doesn't love her anymore. She is finally doing something good with her life and for Kayla. If she lets Mike go, it will all end for her and her little girl. Sheila will probably be glad when Mike's gone. She'll get a great inheritance from his life insurance policy, and Noah will grow up properly without a father to screw up his thinking about women. *I wish he never came here.*

Melanie needs to win over Kayla with this logic. She thinks if she allows the dog to live, even though she hates it, it will help Kayla forgive her.

A distant rumble of thunder.

A storm is rolling in and Melanie is exhausted. Kayla hates storms. She likes to get into bed with her mother when it storms. Melanie prays she will. She listens to the pattering of rain against her window. She opens it and lets the wind and rain blow against her dampening her hair and clothes. The events of the day dissolve--the fresh scent of the air soothes. She lies on the bed and wraps herself in the sheets, creating a cozy nest.

BOOM

That one was close. Brilliant flashes of lightning illuminate Melanie's room--sudden flares of sunlight.The thunder reverberates in her chest. She rolls over with her back toward the door. *Kayla will be coming in any time to join me in bed and cuddle up against me, my back creating a wall of protection against the charged particles of the storm.*

She gazes toward her window. Yellow ochre eyes stare back at her. A flash of lightning illuminates Grimalkin.

Melanie smiles, "My familiar...my guardian angel."

Rumble...crack, BOOM

A creak of the door opening. Melanie can sense her presence. The scent of a child awakened from a dream. Her perspiration pungent with adolescent apprehension.

"Mommy?"

Kayla's sweet voice. "Come into bed, sweetheart." Melanie is pleased, yet she doesn't feel the squish of the mattress give with her daughter's weight. She begins to roll over toward Kayla. "I'll protect you fr..."

CRACK- BOOM!

Grimalkin is in the room standing over Melanie on her bed. Kayla is holding a gun she took from her mother's nightstand and pointing it at the beast. She's shaking violently.

The panther glares at Kayla and growls. Melanie reaches up stroking its muddy front leg. The creature's muscles taut underneath the wet black fur.

"Put the gun down, Honey. There is nothing to be afraid of. My sweet Grimal..."

Grimalkin snaps at Melanie, missing her face by a fraction of an inch. The beast keens.

In the shop, Shep barks wildly, frantically pawing at the door.

BANG! The gun goes off. Kayla screams. Grimalkin leaps out of the window.

*

In the freezer, Mike cowers at the sight of the horse's vibrating torso. It whinnies even though it doesn't have a head. The cadaver of the man hanging on the hook flexes and wiggles his way off of it. He writhes on his legless stumps toward the horse. The horse bucks on his hook and snorts. The cadaver, missing his extremities, leans against it soothing the poor frozen animal. He turns toward Mike. Mike squirms up against the door of the freezer. He's tired and relieved to see someone else in his predicament.

"Good to have someone to talk to," Mike says to the man. "It'll help keep my mind off of the cold, brrrr."

The cadaver bows to him.

"Course since you don't have a head, the conversation has to be one way. I'm mighty curious what happened to you. Did my sister kill you?"

The cadaver twists his torso to indicate "no". It leans on its stumps and falls on its back.

"You fell?"

The cadaver twists and struggles to upright itself, bending at the waist to indicate, "yes".

"Then, my sister did this to you?"

The cadaver bends at the waist again.

"Wow, sorry about what happened to you and all. No offense, but I hope she doesn't do that to me." The air seems to leave cadaver's lungs. His posture crumples. He tries to speak--only the rumble of thunder erupts from his neck. He stands, his torso straight. With his chest and arm stubs he pushes against the door. Mike can see his muscles flex. Mike wants to help him, but he's paralyzed. Cadaver backs up and pushes again. Mike feels himself fading when a beam of intense light filters through the slits of his eyes. The beam grows. He can feel the door moving away from his back. He collapses on the floor.

A huge wet tongue emerges from the neck of the torso and licks Mike's face, gross yet warm. He's wrapped in a cocoon. A distant voice is calling to him..." Uncle Mike...Uncle Mike".

Mike wills his eyes to open. He tries to take a deep breath...a vise on his lungs keeps him from doing so. Looking down at him and licking his face is a dog--not a torso, a dog--a big, furry...Shep! Shep keens a high-pitched whine and rolls up against Mike, his tail wagging furiously. Mike attempts to reach up to pet him, but his arm and brain aren't quite connecting.

The voice again. "Uncle Mike".

Mike rolls his eyeballs away from Shep to the sound. It's Kayla. She is wrapping him in blankets. He realizes he can't move his arm because she has wrapped a blanket tightly around him. He tries to speak, but only a harsh whisper seeps from his parched lips.

"You're alive!" Kayla places a pillow under Mike's head. Millions of tiny needles prick his skin as his body warms. His hands ache.

"Water," Mike moans. He has a screaming headache.

"I made you some warm tea."

"That'll do." Kayla lifts her Uncle Mike's head from the pillow and holds a cup to his lips. Warm fluid drips down his throat, over his lips and down his chin. It feels marvelous. The pain in his chest is abating and he can breathe in a bit deeper, but it makes him cough. He drinks more tea.

"My hands hurt."

Kayla pulls his hands from the blanket. The tips of Mike's fingers are pale. His knuckles have flecks of black and the palms of his hands are riddled with burns from trying to hold the battery. Kayla rubs them with ointment and wraps them in gauze making them hurt more. She gives her uncle some aspirin in hopes they will help. Shep lies next to him and rests his head on Mike's neck. Shep's muscular body under his soft fur and his beautiful face soothes Mike. He begins to doze off.

Kayla worries about letting someone with hypothermia sleep. Her uncle looks so calm and relaxed she lets him be.

BANG, BANG, BANG. Melanie is locked out of the shop and hitting her fists against the door. "Let me in!"

Shep lurches at the door barking viciously. There are sirens in the distance.

Mike wakes. "Wha...?"

Kayla talks so fast, Mike can't understand a word she is saying. "I took Mom's gun and locked her out. Oh, Uncle Mike, I almost shot her. I couldn't stand what she was doing any more. I saw her gun on the nightstand, and when I picked it up, Grimalkin jumped through the window. It was crazy. She almost bit Mom, so I shot at her. I grabbed the keys and ran to save you. The police are on their way...I didn't want you to die," she sobs.

"I'm going to be alright. You're a wonderful nurse."

The sirens stop. The banging stops. Shep's barking stops.

He lopes over to Mike and licks him eagerly.

Banging on the door again. "This is the police!"

Kayla runs to the door and unlocks it. Paramedics rush in and examine Mike. They put an IV into his arm and place him in a stretcher. Detective Billings walks in. Shep approaches him wagging his tail.

"Nice dog." He turns to Mike. "How are you feeling?"

"Man, like a million dollars...pricking my skin." The paramedics are wrapping his hands in fresh gauze.

"Looks like this brave little girl got to you without a minute to spare."

"Yeah, I owe her big time."

Kayla hugs Mike. "I love you, Uncle...uh, Dad."

"We're going to need statements from both of you. It can wait until you're both feeling better. We have Mrs. Miller in custody."

Mike gazes at his wrapped hands, tears in his eyes.

"She's my sister."

"I'm sorry this had to happen to your family. Is there somewhere we can take Kayla?" Detective Billings nods to the EMTs loading Mike into a stretcher.

"Yes, to my home. You can call my wife, Sheila. Kayla knows her number."

Kayla hugs him and begins to sob. Shep whines.

Detective Billings pats Kayla on the shoulder, "He's going to be okay. Let's get ahold of your aunt."

Mike holds Kayla in his numb arms. "You're going home." The EMTs load him into the ambulance and drive away.

*

The routine is the same day after day. Jerry serves his mother dinner on her TV tray while she sits in Pa's recliner. Her eyes seem to glaze over watching one program meld into another one never bothering to use the remote. Pa always used it and neither she nor Jerry knows how to operate it. It happens to be on her favorite soaps and programs so she's content. She never hits the off button, choosing to eat and sleep where she sits with the television constantly on. She only leaves the chair to use the bathroom and hide money. The only conversation with her son is when she has something to yell at him about. Jerry's love for her is unfailing. He walks to the bank and grocery once a month in dedication. Today is different. While walking home, something huge and black runs across the street and disappears behind a house. He is sure it's the panther. Today, Jerry runs home.

Chapter 15

Going Home

Grimalkin runs. She can't return to the woods—they are full of hunters. She can't go back to Tiger World—traps line the entire place. No food has been left for her. She must find her way back to the farm. She finds sustenance from garbage left outside at night, chasing away raccoons who had been dining on people's leftovers. She licks Styrofoam trays to taste small amounts of blood the meat on them left behind. Her stomach cramps. She was used to eating only fresh meat.

She lifts her nose in the air—a familiar smell of meat. It's a smoky scent...but it's meat. Grimalkin follows the aroma toward a celebration. There are strange creatures dancing. Music is playing...and they are eating...meat!

The celebration is The Beast of Bladenboro festival held every year on Halloween in Bladenboro, North Carolina. People are in costumes—many dressed as a panther with a bear's head. The mascot for the festival, a cartoony looking cat, walks around the festival grounds taking pictures with the children and dancing to music. It is all confusing to Grimalkin. She spies the mascot eating a turkey leg. Grimalkin drools, she can't stay away any longer. She creeps out of the woods through the brush toward the strange character. She stops only feet away from him.

"Wow! Would you look at that?" The mascot is amazed. "You will win the contest for sure." He lifts his mask to take a big bite out of the smoked turkey leg and glances about. Grimalkin glares at him. "Where's your owner? The pet costume contest is over there," the mascot waves the turkey leg in the direction of the competition. Grimalkin snarls and pounces at the leg, ripping it out of the mascot's hand. She scats back into the woods.

The mascot stands in place vibrating in fear. "I think I just crapped myself."

The festival grounds turn into chaos as word about the panther sighting spreads. Grimalkin purrs, eating the best meal she's had in ages, unaware Blaine Springer's farm is only a few miles away.

*

"Are you really my father?" Kayla asks.

"Yes," Mike replies.

She sits staring at him for what seems like some contest, and she is winning.

"Why didn't anyone tell me?"

"I was a kid. I was sixteen and living with friends. When my girlfriend got pregnant, she didn't want anything to do with me and her parents pressured her to give the baby up for adoption. Mel jumped at the chance. She was twenty-one and already married to Rob who was stationed in Iraq. It was perfect timing. She had just been told by her doctor becoming pregnant would be nearly impossible because of scar tissue in her uterus caused by trauma. If she did get pregnant, she would most likely lose her baby."

"Trauma?" Kayla asks.

"Like an injury or an infection...something like that."

"Like getting whipped in the stomach with a belt?"

She's taken Mike off guard. "What?"

"Mom told me about your father, about his terrible whipping...then my own father beat her. Poor Mommy," Kayla weeps.

"You made her happy. We were worried about Rob. He never allowed her to have a pet. A child is a much bigger deal. When he came back, we were all afraid he would force Mel to give you up, but he took you in his arms and swore that you would never live the life he did...being shuffled from one foster home to another. I admired him for that."

"Oh, Uncle Mike," Kayla holds him tight and sobs into his shoulder. Mike feels like a father. He wants to protect her and envelopes her in his arms to shield her from this terrible mess. Shep nuzzles them and lies at their feet.

"So many times, I wanted to tell you and take you home with me. Get you away from Rob's violent temper, but Mel needed you. You gave her joy."

Kayla's heart aches. "She isn't my mommy anymore. I saw it in her eyes. Something happened to her to shut off all her sense of what is good and right. Maybe she had a brain injury from one of my dad's beatings. Uncle Mike, she was murdering men and using Grimalkin to get rid of them."

"It was her all along?"

"Yes, and you were running out of time. I crept into her room. Her back was to me. A clap of thunder made me jump. I heard her voice say, "Come into bed, sweetheart." I hesitated a moment. It sounded like Mom. A flash of lightning revealed her gun on the nightstand. I grabbed it.

I was going to shoot her. I didn't want to hurt her. I just wanted her to feel no more pain. I knew she didn't want to end up in prison." Kayla sobs and leans against Shep. He nudges his head under her hand so she will pet him. It's calming. "You were running out of time."

Uncle Mike leads her to the kitchen and pours her a glass of milk.

"That's when Grimalkin jumped through the window. The gun went off. I don't know if I shot it or not. Where is she? What do we do?" Kayla wipes her eyes with the hem of her T shirt.

"I got you, K K. We'll get through this," Mike sits at the kitchen table in deep thought. He takes Kayla's hand into his. He remains like that for what seems like ages. "K K, your mother will get help now."

"What happened to her? She isn't my Mommy any-more."

"It was her mind. It snapped. The abuse she suffered sent her over the edge."

"I had to call the police. I had to stop her. Do you think she hates me now?" Kayla cries.

"Shush," he soothes. "You had to do it. Who knows what more she would have done...who she would hurt...possibly you? She had to be stopped."

Kayla is relieved Uncle Mike is her real father. She was worried that she would develop her dad's temper. Something happened to his mind too. Kayla prays nothing bad will happen to hers. She's seen things no one should see--let alone a fourteen-year-old. She's glad she still has a family. *Hey, I'm Noah's big sister.* The thought makes her smile.

"Where do you think Grimalkin is?"

"I don't know," Mike considers Shep wagging his tail gazing at them. He pats him, "Do you know where the monster is, boy?"

Shep barks happily and chases his tail.

"Shep says we're in the clear." And then the best words Kayla has ever heard, "We're safe at home."

"Can I keep calling you Uncle Mike? It seems weird calling you Dad."

He chuckles, "Sure, no problem."

"And Aunt Sheila, Aunt Sheila?"

Mike laughs, "By the way, Nick's coming by later.

He says he's sorry he didn't get back to you. He had lost his phone.

Tsk, boys!

Chapter 16

Maude

Jerry's mother has stopped walking. When she must use the bathroom, she has Jerry carry her in. When she is finished, she screams for him to fetch her. He dutifully gives her baths. He doesn't know what is wrong with her. Jerry continues to give her medicine with the red dots. He isn't a very good cook, so they count on frozen dinners and canned food. What he is good at is keeping the house in tip top shape. He likes cleaning and fixing things around the house. When he is done, he admires his work...something he did by himself. Ma is watching TV when she slams her glass of iced tea down on her tray, spilling it. Jerry runs into the living room to clean it.

"I knew it," she yells. "I knew it was no panther killing those guys."

Jerry cocks his head to one side in confusion.

Ma leans forward shaking her finger at the TV screen. "Some nutty woman did it all. I tell ya, it's a crazy world when women start killing. It's always been men that done it,"

"Why?" Jerry asks.

"Hell, if I know. Something just went bad in her head, I guess."

Jerry sits down on the sofa watching the news with his mother. He wonders if maybe the world was going too fast for the woman, and she had to strike out. He doesn't know what the world is like with his very limited experience of it. He had asked his mother about the two of them going to the ocean since it made her happy. She said she is too crippled now to even try.

Jerry slumps, his eyes close when Ma interrupts. "I'm getting chilly. Why don't you start a nice fire in the fireplace?"

Jerry's seen the fireplace used once. It was Christmas when he was around six years old. There is wood in it, but it's been there since he was seven. He doesn't know how to use a fireplace. He supposes it's not very hard. Ball up some paper, put it on the wood then light it with a match. He can do that.

While searching for paper to crumple, Jerry turns to his mother. "What...about...the panther? Did...did they...kill it?"

"Nah, it ran off. The idiots have a posse out for the poor thing."

Chapter 17

PART II

Farmer Blaine

Blaine Springer searched for Grimalkin. He put out a nice fat pig every night to attract her. Nothing. He heard about some creature attacking a young man in Denton which surprised him. Denton is over one-hundred and thirty miles away. If that was her, why would she run so far? There were news reports of a body found. They suspected Grimalkin. Farmer Blaine watched the news every night praying she wouldn't be killed.

He continued his attempts to lure the cat with a pig. One year, two months and six days later, the pig disappeared. Blaine heard the familiar high-pitched baby cry of Grimalkin. He ran out to see her steal into the night. She's much easier to see now. Her pitch-black fur is turning steel grey. Her bright yellow eyes have dimmed. She limps...possibly from an injury. His sweet Grimalkin has come home.

Blaine Springer is an old man. It gets harder every day to care for Grimalkin. He needs help. It can't be just anyone. He needs someone who understands. Grimalkin isn't evil—she is only doing what God designed her to do and she's the last of her kind.

Chapter 18

House Afire

"Jerry, get in here. The house is on fire!"

Jerry Pritchard runs into the living room. It is filling up quickly with smoke.

"Idiot! Look what you've done!" She coughs. Her eyes begin to water. Her arms flail about in an attempt to disperse the smoke from her face.

"The damn chimney's on fire. I told you it needed cleaning," she spits. "Call the fire department."

Jerry runs to the wall phone in the kitchen. He picks up the receiver and stares at it. The voice of his loving mother breaks his concentration.

"Dial 911, moron!"

The yard is in total disarray. Weeds have over-taken the garden and several balls lay in waste. Jerry carries his mother out of the house and lets the firemen in. He sets her on the curb. Several neighbors and children step out of their homes to watch the event. No one approaches them. No one speaks to them. Jerry's mother is relieved. She doesn't want to bother with anyone. She nods her head at Jerry and glares toward the firemen going into their house.

"Keep an eye on them. Don't want 'em takin' anything out of there," she orders.

"Yes...Ma'am." Jerry obeys.

"All wrapped up," a fireman calls out to them. "It was just a chimney fire. There's a little smoke damage, but everything else looks pretty good. You gotta clean out your chimney every now and then," he smiles.

Maude closes her eyes to shield herself from having to talk to him.

Jerry swallows hard. "Thank...you."

"Sure, no problem," the fireman reaches out to shake Jerry's hand. Jerry, not knowing what to do, he only shrugs. The fireman retrieves his hand and with a furrow in his brow, begins to leave. "By the way," he calls over his shoulder. "You need to check the basement. I think an animal died down there."

"Oh...kay," Jerry answers and helps his mother back into the house.

His mother lets out a deep sigh once Jerry returns her to the easy chair--the chair that was once her husband's. She even sleeps in it.

She eyes the room. "Look at this place! Clean it up. Get it done before my dinner."

While Jerry cleans, he thinks about his monthly errands to the bank and the grocery store. Ma makes him hide money she gets from the bank around the house. Every so often Ma will give Jerry money to walk the three miles to the Food Lion for bread and milk. He doesn't mind, he likes the smell of rain after it soaks the dry earth, or the aroma of wood burning from someone's fireplace on a crisp day, and even the heat of the summer sun on his skin.

Ma's squawking shakes Jerry out of his thoughts. "Hey, get outta la la land and make me something to eat!" He runs to the kitchen to get going. "And don't forget my pills."

Jerry, fixated on his cooking, neglects to fetch the pills. His mother yells, "Jerry, you hear me?" No answer.

"Jerry! You stupid retard, I'm talking to you. If I have to get them myself, you're gonna regret it."

He jerks to attention and frantically searches for her pills. He has forgotten where they are. In his search Jerry accidentally knocks a carton of milk off of the counter spraying it everywhere.

Ma, after struggling to get out of her chair, limps toward the kitchen. "You really are an imbecile." She slips and falls hard.

"Jerry!" She's splayed out on the floor. "It hurts. I think I did something to my arm. Help me."

"Call 9...1...1?" he asks.

No. No 911. Just help me back into my chair. I'll be all right," She adjusts herself holding her arm. "Holy cow on a cracker, it hurts." She winces. "Get my pain pills. They're in the bathroom cabinet. Bring any pill bottles you find. The rest are in the refrigerator."

He brings back twelve pill bottles. Ma sorts through them like a pro and finds the ones for pain. She swallows several. Jerry brings her a tray of food she gulps down.

"Are...you...okay?" he asks.

"I'll be fine. Just stop blocking the damn TV and leave me alone."

Jerry plods to the attic with his dinner the way he has always done since he was a child. The next morning, the television is shouting a commercial for some car scratch stuff. *Rub it on, buff it out. It makes your car look brand new.* He takes a furtive step into the room, Ma's sitting there all still, peaceful almost. The commercial woke Jerry. He slept in and he's late with her meds. He's afraid Ma's revving up to yell at him.

"Ma?" Jerry calls quietly. He doesn't want to startle her, or he'll have Hell to pay. "Ma?"

No response. *Is she so mad she won't talk to me?* He taps her on the shoulder. She feels cold. He faces her and gazes into her eyes. No emotion in them-nothing. A huge lump finds its way into his throat.

"Ma?" He sobs, "Ma!"

He kneels at her feet and lays his head in her lap. His heart has a pain he never knew before. *She counted on me. She counted on me to take care of her. I can't even take care of my Ma.* Jerry wraps a blanket over her shoulders and sits watching her with the television blaring for the rest of the day, waiting for her to suddenly wake up and yell at him again.

Several days later with Ma still in her chair, developing the same familiar smell that wafts from the basement, Jerry sits at the kitchen table gazing at the photo of his parents on their honeymoon at the ocean. Ma often talked fondly about the beach. She said the ocean is so big that you can't see land on the other side. She could feel and breathe in the salty wave-born mist and walk barefoot in the sand. Her times at the ocean were the best of their lives until Jerry was born. They didn't go anywhere then. Ma often mentioned to Pa that they should go to the beach. Pa never answered her.

Jerry fills a paper sack with money and peanut butter sandwiches. "I...am...going...to the beach."

Chapter 19

The Walk

Jerry stops in the doorway and gazes at the outdoors in front of him. He never left the house without his mother's permission. The air seems different to him this morning—fresher, and brisk. He takes in a deep breath, definitely better than the inside air. A thought occurs to him. He retreats into the house and picks up the photo of his parents he left on the kitchen table. They are young and happy, hand in hand, with the surf behind them. Jerry carefully places the photo in his paper bag. Walking toward the door he glances back at his mother, still in her husband's easy chair.

"Good-bye...Mama. I...hope you...go to heaven." Jerry steps outside of his home and stops on the sidewalk outside of the gate unsure which direction he should go. He stands very still and closes his eyes. The wind brushes against his back and rustles his hair, seeming to push him, so he walks that way...east.

He walks along with the giddy beat of his heart. He should be afraid. He doesn't have his mother to tell him where to go or what to do. She always told him he was too stupid to decide for himself—yet, here he is, walking away from everything he's ever known. He begins to lope instead of walk. It's a new world he can't wait to meet.

*

Kayla clocks into work at McDonald's in Rockwell, North Carolina. Being fifteen she feels she should work part time to help out with expenses at home. Uncle Mike and Aunt Sheila have been great, and she babysits little Noah every chance she gets. Working at McDonald's not only gives her a way to help out, but she can also be more independent and besides, it's fun.

"Hey, Sarah," Kayla dons her Micky D cap. She is happy her best friend works there as well.

"Hi." Sarah is concentrating on the machine that dispenses the frappes, fidgeting with the pitcher and shoving it under the dispenser. She pounds on the buttons. It makes a horrible grinding noise. "Ugh! I can't get this damn thing to work. I hate it," she yells, and kicks the machine.

"Let me see what's up with it."

"Go right ahead, be my guest," Sarah waves to the machine.

Kayla grabs a stool and stands up on it in order reach the ice hopper lid. She opens it and looks inside.

"Oh, crap! They didn't clean out the machine last night. The ice melted, then froze again. Now, it's one big chunk of ice."

"Shit, now what?"

"We gotta unplug it and wait for it to thaw out enough to break up and put fresh ice in there."

"Oh, my Gawd, that will take hours!"

"Shhh, we just can't sell any frappes for a while." Kayla unplugs the machine.

"Tell them," Sarah points to three very annoyed women with hands on their hips and scrunched up faces.

Kayla wonders which one is in charge of the eye of Newt.

*

After several hours of walking, Jerry is hungry. He ate his peanut butter sandwiches five minutes after he left the house. Knowing they were in his bag made him want to eat them. His feet ache too. He needs a rest. It was hard when he ran out of sidewalk and walked along the road. He was honked at several times. He waved, but no one waved back except for one guy who Jerry supposed was using sign language. The guy made a fist at him with his middle finger held straight up in the air.

Jerry wasn't sure what the guy meant—maybe he was saying, "Look up". He did, but he didn't see anything 'cept for a few clouds. He spies McDonald's golden arches down the street. He knows they sell food because his parents ate a lot of it. His pa would say, "I'm goin' to the golden arches." He would come back with hamburgers and fries and milkshakes. Jerry always got a kids meal—even as recently as the day before his dad died. That day he thought he saw the panther run past the drive through.

He's a grown-up now. Grown-ups eat big hamburgers.

He opens the door and three women burst out of the building brushing past him and sounding like hens all clucking at once. They aren't happy which confuses Jerry. "The...golden arches...is a happy...place." "Screw you!" one of the women yells. Now, he's really confused.

He approaches the register Sarah is manning. Kayla is putting away the stool.

"Can I help you?" Sarah is polite and smiling.

"Hmmm," Jerry squints at the menu board. He can't read. He studies the pictures of food while tightly gripping a paper bag in his arms.

"I...wa...want...a ham...burger."

"What kind?"

"Meat. I...want...one with meat," he proudly answers.

"I mean, do you want a cheeseburger, quarter pounder, Big Mac, Bacon Smokehouse Burger, or a triple burger?" Sarah' words slur together sounding like,

"Cheequarterpounmacbaconsmoketriple...burger." Jerry doesn't understand her, but remembers his mother always got two cheeseburgers, no pickle. "Two...cheese-burgers...no...pickle."

"Full meal deal?" Jerry nods.

"Large fries and a Coke?" Sarah continues.

Jerry nods.

"That'll be eight dollars and fifty-seven cents."

Jerry leans on one foot and then the other. He doesn't know how to count out money. Ma always did that for him. He hopes he has enough in his bag. He filled it about half-way with the money he found stashed around the house. He sets the bag on the counter and opens it. He removes the photo of his parents.

"Can you...just take...what...you need?" he asks.

Sarah leans over and gazes into the bag. There are easily thousands of dollars in it. The bills are mostly twenties with a few fifties sprinkled in. She gingerly reaches inside and takes a twenty. She rings it up and drops the change into the bag.

"You took...only one...and...and then...gave me more?" Jerry is amazed.

"Uh, I only needed eight dollars. You have like thousands in there. I gave you change." She hands him an empty cup. His mother always gave him a full cup of soda.

"What's this...for?" He holds the empty cup upside down.

Sarah points to the drink machines. Kayla notices Jerry's confusion, "I'll help him out." She walks around the counter and leads him to the machine.

Jerry is in awe at all of the flavors of drinks. His ma always told him there was just Coke.

"What would you like?" Kayla smiles sweetly presenting the machine like a hostess in a game show.

"Can...I get a...orange?"

"Sure," Kayla takes his cup and pushes it against the ice machine lever. The frozen water cubes clunk into his cup. Then she puts the cup under the orange soda dispenser and pushes the lever with the cup. Neon orange soda pours into it. Jerry steps back with his mouth agape. She places a plastic lid on the full cup and picks up a straw. "I'll take this to your table for you. Where would you like to sit?"

Jerry scans the dining room. It's lunchtime in the middle of the week and several men wearing orange vests sit at tables. He spots a small one by the window away from the men and points to it.

Kayla walks to the table and sets his drink down. "Have a seat, we'll bring your food to you," she smiles.

He sits and a few moments later, Sarah arrives with his meal. "There ya go. Enjoy."

Kayla and Sarah go back to the counter while Jerry unwraps his first cheeseburger. The bag sits in his lap.

Sarah grabs Kayla's arm.

"Did you look in his bag? There is like, thousands in it. I think he robbed a bank or something."

Kayla glances over her shoulder at him. "He doesn't seem to be the type to do that."

"Something is up. No one walks around with a paper bag full of money. We gotta call the cops."

"You think?"

Sarah nods her head vigorously.

They both look back at Jerry. He smiles at them with a mouth full of cheeseburger.

Chapter 20

"Dirty Bully Pigs"

Sarah meets officers Kent and Braden at the door of the restaurant and quietly tells them about Jerry's bag of money. By now, Jerry has finished his meal. He stands to gather his things when the officers approach him.

Jerry's mother often told him that the police are nothing but pigs—dirty bully pigs. *They get near you and WHAM, they beat you, put you in the slammer and take all your money.* Jerry doesn't know for sure what a slammer is, but he knows what slam means, and that hurts. Her words drilled into his head.

Jerry screams in fright, frozen in fear. He grabs his bag and wills himself to run. The officers catch him and easily pin him to the ground. Money and the photo of his parents, spill onto the floor.

"Don't...slam...me...p...please!"

"Now, calm down. Nobody wants to slam you."

Jerry is face down on the floor with Officer Kent's knee pushing on his back.

Jerry continues to flail. Kayla picks up the bag and its contents.

"Just leave it. Back up and let us do our work, okay?" Officer Braden demands.

Kayla lays the bag down and backs up. Jerry is sobbing making her regret calling the police. By now, everyone in the restaurant is watching the literal floor show.

"If you don't calm down, I'm going to have to hurt you. Stop now!"

Jerry stops at Officer Kent's loud command, but his heart doesn't. It's crawling up his throat to jump out and run home without him.

"Shhh, you're going to be alright. If you promise to shut up and sit quietly, I'll take my knee off of you...got it?"

Jerry nods. Officer Kent stands. Rolling to a sitting position on the floor, legs splayed out in front of him, snot oozes from his nose and curls around Jerry's upper lip, finding its way into his mouth. Kayla passes a napkin to Officer Kent to give to him.

"Here, clean that sh...stuff off of your face."

Jerry blows his nose. Officer Kent squats in front of him. Officer Braden stands with Jerry's bag and counts the money on a nearby table.

"Now listen. We don't want to hurt you...hell, we don't even want to arrest you. We just want to know why you're walking around with a paper bag full of money."

"There's over a hundred-thousand dollars here." Officer Braden shouts.

"That's a heck of a lot of change there, boy.
Where'd it come from?"

"Home," Jerry sniffs. "It's...my...ma's. She...she let me...have it."

"She did, huh? Where ya headin' with it?"

"The...beach."

Officer Kent nods, still squatting on the floor. "Tell ya what, why don't we go visit you mom first? Then, you can go to the beach." He stands and pulls Jerry to his feet.

"She...uh...she's sleeping," Jerry's heart is searching for an escape route again.

"We promise not to stay long. You know your address?"

Jerry nods.

"Then, let's go," Officer Kent leads Jerry out the door followed by Officer Braden holding Jerry's paper bag.

Sarah and Kayla stand motionless gazing out the door. Watching Jerry get into the police car, an image of a bull loaded into a trailer comes to Kayla's mind. *Is the driver taking him to slaughter?*

"What kind of mom would give someone like Jerry all that cash?" Sarah muses. "Maybe I should get to know him better."

Kayla playfully slaps Sarah on the arm. "Sarah, there is obviously something wrong with him. I feel bad. I mean, that officer had his knee on Jerry's neck. He wasn't going to hurt anyone."

"He was trying to run away."

"Well, he wasn't running very fast in those beat up tennies. They looked like he walked a thousand miles in them. If his family was really rich, wouldn't he have better shoes?" Kayla points at her feet.

"That's why I think he robbed somebody, or something like that. We did the right thing by calling the cops. Some guys that look harmless are the ones who you gotta watch for." Sarah trots to her station at the counter while a customer walks up.

Kayla places a hand on the door, watching the police car drive away. "His eyes were kind. I think something terrible happened to him, and we just made it worse."

*

By the time the officers pull up to Jerry's home it is dark. The house is dark as well. The stark brick exterior surrounded by the tall chain-link fence gives it the appearance of a prison. The officers exit their car locking Jerry in the back seat. Officer Kent slowly opens the gate. It makes a loud metallic whine. He gently taps on the door.

"Mrs. Pritchard?" he calls out.

Nothing.

He knocks on the door.

Nothing.

He bangs on the door.

Nothing.

He tries the doorknob. It turns easily. A rancid odor hits the men in the face as the door opens.

Officer Braden covers his nose with the sleeve of his jacket. "What died in here?" He whispers.

"I know this stench," Officer Kent remembers a time he had walked into a drug den to find four people rotting on a couch. They had been there for weeks, all had OD'd. The smell is similar to spoiled chicken...only a hundred times worse. He threw up then. He feels the contents of his stomach coming up now and rushes to the side of the front steps to release them.

"Do we really have to go in there?" The only visible parts of Officer Braden's face are his worried eyes; his eyebrows resembling an upside-down V.

"No. Let's keep Rain Man in the station overnight and let homicide check it out in the morning."

"Good idea."

Chapter 21

Miranda Rights

"You have the right to remain silent. Anything you say can be used against you in a court of law. You have the right..."

"Wait...wait...what's...happening? Why...?"

"To talk to a lawyer for advice before..."

"A...a lawyer? Why?" Jerry pleads. He is sitting in a temporary jail cell while the officer continues to read him his Miranda rights.

"We ask you any question. If you cannot afford a lawyer..."

"I can't. You...took...you took...my money."

"One will be appointed for you before any questioning if you wish. If you decide to answer questions now without a lawyer present, you have the right to stop answering at any time. Do you understand?"

Homicide had entered Jerry's home early this morning-- the stink inking through their masks. Jerry's mother sat right where he left her. A puddle of liquid had oozed from her to the chair and onto the floor, a melting candle. Her mouth hung open; her teeth had fallen out onto her lap. Her eye sockets were dark and hollow. The ambulance attendants had a hard time putting her into a body bag.

Her loose wet skin kept slipping through their gloved fingers.

Searching the home, the officers found wads of cash hidden throughout the house—a thousand under her chair, ten thousand under mattresses, thirty thousand in a flour canister in the kitchen cabinet, ten thousand in a plastic bag hidden in the water reserve of a toilet, thirty thousand in the freezer of their refrigerator, and a stack of twenties in the end table totaling fifty thousand. It was a great treasure hunt—until the detectives went into the basement. There, under the stairs, was Jerry's father. It was time to read Jerry his Miranda rights. Soon, the discovery of the bodies and the money, $280,000 in total, is spread all over the news.

"That's him! That's the guy at McDonald's," Kayla shouts pointing at the TV to her Uncle Mike who is cleaning up dinner dishes.

"Seriously? Man, that dude murdered his parents to get their money they had stashed all over the house." Mike walks into the living room drying his hands on a dishtowel.

"It doesn't make sense. He didn't seem like that to me, in fact, he was kinda dumb. He didn't know how to pay for his meal."

"Yeah, but his bag was full of money."

"There was also a picture of his parents in it. Would you carry around a picture of your parents if you killed them?"

"All I'm saying is they found his father all chopped up in the basement," Mike shrugs.

"I didn't hear that on the news."

"I saw it on Facebook. It's a fact."

"I think there's more to it. I feel bad for the guy."

"Kayla, you, and Sarah did the right thing by calling the police. They'll take over from here. You stay out of it."

"Hmm," Kayla's thoughts whir like the wings of cicadas. *There's more to the story.* "What do you think, Shep?" The dog gazes at the image of Jerry on the TV screen wagging his tail. "I agree." Kayla smiles and rubs Shep's haunches. He loves it, pushing his rear against her hand smiling a doggy grin.

*

Jerry is sitting across a table from someone he has never seen before. He seems to be a nice man in a nice suit. He has a nice smile. He shakes Jerry's hand and introduces himself as Bob Needing. He's been assigned to Jerry as his public defender.

"Let's see what we got here," Bob pulls a file from his briefcase. Jerry sits quietly unsure what all the fuss is about.

"The coroner's report states your mother likely died from natural causes. That's good...but your father," Bob pauses, reading. He clicks his tongue. "Wow, now that's another story."

"Story? I...don't..."

"You rolled him up in Saran Wrap, huh? Were you the one who administered the poison?"

"What?"

"*Gave* it to him. Your father was poisoned...tetrahydrozoline—a chemical found in eye drops. Not bad in your eyes, but lethal if swallowed. Funny, they would have missed it since your Pa had a bad heart, but since you had to..."

"No! No...poison. He...he took...medicine. He was...sick."

"Did you give him his medicine?"

"Ma...did."

"Well," Bob smiles and leans back in his chair.

"Looks like your ma gave him more than just medicine. Now why, do you suppose, would she do that?"

Jerry can't believe what he's hearing. The question buzzes in his brain. Sweat beads on his forehead at the realization he never really saw Ma happy. That's why the photo is important to him. She was happy once. She would tell him he was the reason she was miserable. "No. Mama...was mean...but...but not..." He stops abruptly and thinks for a moment. "She...she didn't like...the names."

"Names?"

"Yeah...Pa called her...a...an ugly...old...Grim...Grimal-kin...yeah...that's it," Jerry's proud he remembers the name. Pa called her other names, but Grimalkin really jazzed her.

"Grimalkin?"

Jerry nods at Bob vigorously.

"That's from Shakespeare. It means old spiteful woman, or grey female cat."

"Shake...Shakespeare is a...old...spiteful...woman?"

"No, no. He was a writer. He told stories. Grimalkin is from one he wrote called "Macbeth." One of the witches used the term.

"Yeah? He...called her...a...witch too."

Bob chuckles. "Did your father read?" Jerry shrugs.

"You don't know if he read?"

"I...was in...my room."

Bob gazes at Jerry in amazement of what this couple did to their own flesh and blood. "Jerry, since you never gave your pa his "medicine", that's going to put you in the clear. Now, we gotta talk about your "abuse of a corpse" charge. Why did you tuck him under the basement stairs? You had the money for a funeral." Bob is writing on a yellow pad.

"Ma...told me...to. She...she didn't...want any...anyone to know..."

"That he died?"

Jerry nods.

A realization jogs up to Bob and slaps him in the head. "Wait a minute. You said you walked to the bank once a month?"

Jerry nods.

"Huh, I get it now. She was cashing in your father's Social Security checks!"

Jerry blinks at Bob. He doesn't know what it all means.

"Son, we're going to clear this whole thing up. You'll be free in no time." Bob smiles, stands, grabs Jerry's hand, and shakes it. It feels like some kind of weird ceremony to Jerry.

He saw guys do that on TV. *So that's what the fireman was trying to do. Guys shake hands because they don't hug and kiss each other.*

"Will...will I...get my...bag back?"

"Nope, that belongs to the state. You'll get your picture back and you'll be getting your own Social Security money in a few months." Bob considers Jerry a moment realizing Jerry has nowhere to go. "The court will come up with a living arrangement for you in the meantime...okay?"

Jerry nods, unsure of what he's agreeing to.

Chapter 22

Living Arrangements

Jerry stands in front of a large two-story house. Most of the paint has chipped away from its wood siding. A tattered blue tarp flaps in the wind on the roof—abandoned since volunteers tacked it over missing shingles caused by the last hurricane.

Two young men sit in kitchen chairs on the front porch, their drab clothing matching the siding. They're smoking and laughing.

Jerry hugs his framed photograph close to his chest—his only possession now.

"You'll be fine," the social worker calls out from her little Ford Fiesta. "They're nice guys." She tosses a paper bag out of the car window toward Jerry. "Here. The girls at the office got you a few things to wear. I'll keep in touch...okay?"

No sooner does Jerry nod, his social worker drives away, leaving him alone. He wants to go to the beach— not live with a bunch of guys he doesn't know. As he begins to walk away, one of the men on the porch whistles at him and motions for him to come. Not one to disobey orders, Jerry picks up his bag and walks toward the group home.

The young man who whistled stands, throws his cigarette over the railing, and extends his hand to Jerry. Knowing the ceremony now, Jerry takes the man's hand and shakes it.

"So, you're the new guy, huh?"

"I...guess...so."

"I'm the den father here, name's Frank." He smiles, showing Hollywood white teeth. Jerry is mesmerized.

"Hi, Fr...Frank. My...name...is..." Jerry is gazing at Frank's teeth, wondering how he got them so clean.

"Jerry," Frank interrupts. "Nice to meet ya. I'm supposed to give you special attention here. I'm gonna give you a guided tour."

"Thank...you," Jerry smiles slightly, feeling self-conscience of his own teeth.

Frank points at his eyes laughing. "Hey bud, my eyes are up here."

The other guy on the porch laughs out loud. Jerry obeys the order, his face hot. His ma used to slap him for staring.

Frank leads Jerry into the house. "This here is our living room."

This place looks nothing like the only home he's ever known. Two men are sitting in the room. One is sprawled out on the tattered sofa snoring and the other one is sitting in an overstuffed chair watching WWF wrestling on the small flat screen TV. Chip bags, empty soda cans, and cigarette butts litter the room.

"Sorry about that," Frank apologizes. "We keep asking for a bigger TV."

Jerry gives him the side eye. Mama would have knocked him into next week if she found her living room in this state. Frank shows Jerry the rest of the house. There are two bathrooms in desperate need of cleaning and a kitchen with dishes scattered everywhere. The range top appears to be rarely used and the microwave...let's just say that's where all the cooking is happening. Finally, Jerry is shown his room.

Frank waves over the dismal furnishings. First prize in Wheel of Fortune. "This is your room. You gotta share it with Rick. He's a good guy. I think you'll get along with him." He nods toward a corner of the dark musty room to a bare, stained mattress on the floor. "That's your bed."

Jerry is used to sleeping on a mattress on the floor, but he's never shared a room with anyone before.

Frank can see Jerry's hesitation. "We got four bedrooms here, but we got six other guys and Joe has to have his own room."

"Joe?"

"You'll get to know him soon enough. Oh, yeah, I bet you'd like some sheets." Jerry nods.

Frank opens a hall cabinet and hands Jerry dingy sheets. "There ya go," he smiles.

"Pillow?"

Frank clicks his tongue and scans the room. The other bed has two pillows. He picks one up and tosses it at Jerry. Jerry, his arms full of sheets and his bag of clothing misses it.

"There...you got your pillow. Anything else Master?" Frank bows.

Jerry shakes his head.

"Good...now," Frank claps his hands together. "No alcohol or smoking is allowed in this house. They find out, you're out! No fighting neither. We have a phone downstairs you can use...and we take turns cleaning once a week. It's your turn this week. Got it?"

Finally, good news. Jerry can't wait to begin cleaning. He nods with a huge smile plastered to his face. Frank wonders what kind of nut they sent to live with him.

*

Sarah rushes into work at Mc Donald's and runs to Kayla who's prepping the frappe machine. "Kayla, Jerry is free!"

"What?" Kayla turns away from the machine releasing the lever too fast, frappe splashes onto her hand.

"They let Jerry go. He's living in a group home now. My mom knows his social worker," Sarah hands Kayla a paper towel.

"Where?" This information is much more interesting than prep. Kayla wipes her hands on the towel.

"In Durham. A place called "New Destinations"
...I think."

"A group-home? Oh, man, that is no place for someone like Jerry. We need to get him out of there." A hope for a second chance and adventure cause the wheels in Kayla's brain to whir, pushing out work and inserting ideas.

"What? Are you kidding me? He's mentally...well, you barely know him. Are you crazy?" Sarah knows that look; Kayla's about to have some nutty plan and she's going to be an accomplice. It breaks the monotony.

"I felt so bad calling the police. All Jerry wanted to do was go to the beach. Now, he's in some group home filled with who knows what, his money is gone, his parents are dead, he's mentally slow, he can't talk right, and he has no one, no friends. Those guys at the group home will eat him alive."

"So, what can we do about it?"

"I have an idea," Kayla smiles wryly.

Bingo! Sarah knew it.

*

Jerry is happily finishing the dishes when one of the group home residents enters the kitchen.

"Damn, lookit this place," he says in wonder at the spotless surfaces. "Ain't you somethin'."

"Th...thank you...I think," Jerry places a plate in its rightful place in the cupboard.

"Th...thank you?" the man mimics. "You stutter?"

"My...words...don't come out...as...fast...as

I...think them."

"Sucks to be you. Hey, I'm Rick, your roommate," Rick smiles and waves.

Jerry nods back, "Jerry." He sticks his hand out to shake Rick's, but he opens the refrigerator instead.

Rick stands at the open door. "What's to eat in here, I'm starving."

"I can...fry up...some eggs."

"Go for it. You the man, Jerry." He sits at the table to wait.

"Thank...you." Jerry gets eggs and bread out of the refrigerator. He put the bread in it because he remembered his ma said it won't grow mold in the refrigerator and he already had to throw some of the bread out. Dusty mold ringed the crust.

Rick raises an eyebrow at Jerry. "Keep the bread in the fridge, huh?"

Jerry nods, searching cabinets for something.

Rick points at the top of the refrigerator. "The toaster's up there."

"Thanks." He reaches for the toaster and places it on the counter. It's dusty with blackened bread crumbs throughout the insides. He carries it to a trashcan to dump out the burnt remnants.

"What the frick?" someone yells from the living room. "What happened to this room? Where is the damn remote?"

Jerry drops the toaster back on the counter. He and Rick rush into the living room. Another resident is throwing the cushions of the couch on the floor. The living room is clean—the cigarette butts, cans, and clothes are gone.

"That's Joe," Rick whispers to Jerry. "You don't want to piss him off. He's been a bear ever since he quit drinking."

"It's...on the side...table!" Jerry points.

Joe stops what he's doing and looks. There it sits. It almost blends into the finish of the dark wood of the table.

"You do this?" Joe shouts at Jerry waving his arm toward the room.

Jerry nods.

"Well, it sucks. If I wanted to live with my Grandma I woulda done so. I like where I sit lived in."

"Lived...in?"

Joe approaches him and now is inches from Jerry's face. "Yeah—lived...duh...in! Now where the frick is my ashtray?"

"No...no smoking...in the..." Jerry begins, when Joe grabs him by the throat with one hand.

"Joe, come on." Rick takes a step forward. "The guy means well. Where is it, Jerry?

Jerry points to the side table gasping for the breath Joe is choking out of him. Rick opens a drawer and pulls out an ashtray. "Here it is," Rick proclaims. He sets it on the distressed coffee table. "Now, please, let him go."

Joe tosses Jerry onto the floor, his elbow banging the corner of the coffee table. Jerry lies there rubbing his elbow.

"Now, Joe, was that necessary?"

"Hmph! Tell your retarded boyfriend to stay outta my way."

"I...I heard...you." That word his mother called him. It's not a nice word. She always said it when he didn't do things right. This time, he wishes he could sock the guy in the nose. He narrows his eyes glaring at Joe.

"Kiss my big fat ass," Joe calmly answers, and kicks Jerry out of the way. He heads for the couch, tosses a cushion back on it, plops down, and begins surfing channels with the remote.

Rick helps Jerry to his feet. "Come on, buddy. We got breakfast to make."

After cleaning the house all day, dealing with Mean Joe Green, and making breakfast out of whatever he could find, Jerry looks forward to some peace and quiet in his room. He had thoroughly cleaned his side and rewashed the bedding. Upon entering, he finds his bed a mess. Ashes and the remains of some kind of cigarette are spread all over the bed and floor. Big, grimy boot prints are ground into his fresh sheets. Rick follows him inside.

"What...happened?" Jerry is aghast.

"Uh, I had some company," Rick kicks an empty soda can aside.

"Why...does it...smell like a...skunk...in here?" Rick shrugs and smiles sheepishly.

Jerry begins to clean all over again.

Chapter 23

The Breakout

"Uncle Mike knows a farmer who's desperate for good help," Kayla opens her register.

"I don't think we should get involved," Sarah wipes down the tables. It's the tenth time Kayla had an idea about what they can do for Jerry.

"It would be a great place for him. It's halfway between here and the ocean. Once Jerry finishes work there, he can go to the beach. Maybe we could all go for a weekend."

Sarah stops what she's doing and glares at Kayla. "Whoa, whoa, whoa. Spend a weekend...with him? You are out of your mind."

"Nicky will drive."

"Oh, great," Sarah rolls her eyes, "Now it's a double date and Jerry's mine."

"No," Kayla laughs, "It's just friends...hanging out."

"Right."

"Anyway, I just think he would do a lot better on the farm. Your mom works at social services. She can tell Jerry's social worker about it and get him a job there. I'll bet you ten dollars he'll want to go."

"Fine, I'll tell her. Give me the info...but I'm not so sure the state will want someone like him alone on a farm with some old dude. I'm just sayin'," Sarah resumes her work. "If I get my Mom to do it, will it shut you up?"

*

"I'm of...sound...mind," Jerry smiles. He's being escorted from the group home by his social worker.

Rick spots him and rushes over. "What the...where are you going?"

Jerry stops and shakes Rick's hand. "I got...a...a job."

"Ya did, huh?" Rick blocks the social worker at the door. "What about me? I'm of sound mind." "It's farm labor," she answers deadpan.

"Oh, screw that," Rick moves out of the way.

"Heh, have a good time, my man."

Jerry beams, "I will."

"Good riddance," shouts Joe from his spot on the couch.

"Oh, yeah? And who's gonna cook for us now?" Jerry hears Rick say behind him. He opens the social worker's car door and squeezes himself into the seat.

"I...have a ...sound...mind," Jerry repeats smiling wide. He's always wanted to live on a farm and care for the animals there. He'll work hard so that the farmer will want him to stay. He knows he'll be good at it. The social worker told him he's of sound mind.

"Don't ask questions, and do as you're told," she drives. "You'll get free room and board, and an allowance for any extras you may need."

Jerry nods.

"Remember, just do what you're told, and you'll have no trouble."

Jerry nods again. Mama taught him to keep his mouth shut and do what he's told. "No...questions."

"Good."

The social worker drives up a long lane with tobacco growing on one side and oats on the other.

Before them is Blaine Springer's farm. His tin-roofed house with a wrap-around porch is dwarfed by the huge red barn on the property and surrounding pastures.

Blaine steps forward to greet the car. Jerry jumps out before the motor is shut off. He grabs the farmer's hand and shakes it vigorously giving the farmer big ceremony.

"Hi...I'm Jerry," trying his best to combine words.

"Blaine Springer. Most folks call me Farmer Blaine."

"Okay," Jerry nods. He has lightness in his head he never felt before. It must be the fresh air. He breathes in deeply and hops over his bag of clothes the social worker dropped on the ground. He spins around scooping it up. He wants to dance. He wants to see the animals. He wants to clean. Oh, so much to see!

The social worker takes Blaine Springer aside. She's talking low to him. Jerry hopes she's telling Farmer Blaine that he's of sound mind. Blaine smiles knowingly at Jerry. He approaches Jerry and pats him on his back.

"Let me show you around, Jerry. Welcome to Springer Farm."

It's the happiest day of Jerry's life.

Chapter 24

New Digs

Jerry sits in the living room of his home at the farm. It's a small cement block shack with a covered porch and a tin roof. In front of him is a small TV on a milk crate. In the kitchen area he rummages in the mini fridge for something to drink—nothing, and no food either. He explores the cabinet beside the dirty sink and finds a few dishes. There are forks and spoons in another drawer as well. At least he'll have something to eat off of when he does get food. Jerry reaches in his bag, pulls out the photo of his parents at the beach and places it on the table. He walks into his bedroom in the back and smooths the sheets on the twin bed. The palms of his hands come up covered with dust. He takes the sheet off of the bed and shakes it outside. Jerry is glad he has a bathroom with indoor plumbing, but he could plant a garden in the mold that has grown in a corner of the shower which has a torn plastic curtain draped in front of it. The floors are badly stained linoleum. Jerry can't wait to start. He'll have it clean in no time...that is if he can find cleaning supplies, and he'll be the only one living there. That's what grownups do.

He picks up the remote to watch television. He knows how to use it from watching his pa. Ma wouldn't let him touch it. He hits the buttons of the remote. The TV works, but only two stations come in...QVC network and WWF wrestling. *Farmer Blaine says he'll call me in for supper about five o'clock. I'm not sure when that is.* After a while of watching QVC network, "Soup's on!" enters loud and clear through his open door.

It's Farmer Blaine! Jerry quickly clicks off the TV and runs toward the house.

*

Jerry is finishing his third bowl of beef vegetable soup when Farmer Blaine tells him they have a big job to do tomorrow. The day after, Jerry can go into town with him for food and supplies.

"You need a cell phone too. I ain't yelling all over the farm when I need you." Farmer Blaine picks up his empty soup bowl and places it in the sink.

Jerry nods. His social security check should come soon and not only will he get a cell phone, but he can get some things like a rug, blanket, and pillow for his new house. Farmer Blaine hands Jerry some fresh sheets for his bed and tells him he'll be by early the next morning. Jerry plants his face into the folded sheets inhaling deeply. The expression on his face is complete ecstasy. The look baffles Farmer Blaine. He guides Jerry out the door with a gentle push on the back.

Crossing the yard toward his home, he feels he's being watched, making him uneasy. After dark, the surroundings seem sinister. A high-pitched wail similar to the cats he's heard in his old neighborhood, only ten times louder sounds close. Jerry runs the rest of the way to his door. He fumbles with the handle. Trees rustle and snap in the woods behind his shack. He turns the knob. In haste, he pulls—he can't get in. A low growl seems to be at his back as he pushes the door. It flies open and he falls into the house. He slams the door shut and pushes a chair against it.

Silence, except for the beating of his heart in his ears. He backs away from the door still holding his sheets. He's afraid to look out the window in fear whatever it is will jump in after him. He sits facing the door, watching intently, and doesn't notice a cockroach scuttle in front of his feet.

*

BAM, BAM, BAM! Jerry jerks awake to the noise. It's daylight.

"Rise and shine, cowboy. We got work to do," shouts Farmer Blaine through the door. "Open up, I have something for you."

Jerry moves the chair blocking the door and opens it.

"How ya like your new digs? Ain't fancy, but at least you got somewhere to sleep," Farmer Blaine steps into the shack.

"I...like it...a lot," Jerry smiles, even though something chased him home last night. He decides not to tell Farmer Blaine about it. He doesn't want to get fired right after getting a job and besides, maybe he was hearing things.

"Good—hey, you need this," Farmer Blaine holds up a flip cell phone. "It's old, but it still works. I already programmed my number in there for ya. You flip it open and at the bottom here it says contacts," he demonstrates. "Then, tap on the line below it like this," he taps. Jerry's eyes grow wide. "Now, see the white plus sign there in the red?"

Jerry nods.

"See, it's surrounded by blue...meanin' it's ready...so tap the OK button here." Farmer Blaine taps again. "See my name there?"

Jerry nods.

"It's surrounded by blue, right?"

"Y...yeah."

"Hit, *send*. It's here on the left." Just after Farmer Blaine taps it, his phone begins ringing in his pocket...a loud, old-time ring. "See there? That's me. Now, to end the call, hit *end* here on the right." He taps on a button on the cell phone, and it quits ringing. "Got it?"

Jerry hesitates a moment, then nods slightly.

"Here," Farmer Blaine hands Jerry the phone.

"Try it."

Jerry never owned something like this before. It fit in the palm of his hand perfectly. It's smooth like steel. He caresses it amazed at what a small, dark object like...

"Hello? Are you gonna stare at it all day?"

Jerry chuckles and flips the phone open. He's giddy about learning a new skill. He remembers to hit the line on the right. Amazingly the white plus sign in the red square is there. He taps on the screen...nothing.

"No, see here...you gotta tap the OK button in the middle," Farmer Blaine explains.

Jerry listens and taps on it. He sees Farmer Blaine's name. He supposes it is since he can't read. Farmer Blaine seems happy. Jerry's finger hovers over the *send* and *end* buttons. *This one or that one?*

Farmer Blaine can't stand it any longer and points at the *send* button. Jerry taps on it. Farmer Blaine's phone begins ringing. He flips his phone open and holds it to his ear. He points at Jerry to do the same.

"Quit foolin' around and get to work," Farmer Blaine yells into his phone.

The farmer's voice in the phone and in front of him echo in Jerry's ears. He immediately puts the phone down and lowers his head. He's being yelled at. He was hoping he wouldn't anger Farmer Blaine. He will probably be kept in the attic now, or worse yet, be sent back to the group home.

Farmer Blaine closes his phone. "What got into you all sudden?"

"You...are...angry. I'm...sorry."

"Oh, hell no son, I was just foolin' with you. I had to say something on the phone. I'm not mad...yet." Farmer Blaine chuckles. "Listen here. When I call, just flip your phone open and listen, got it?"

Jerry nods as the air escapes his lungs in relief.

"Good. Now, get yourself cleaned up. Got breakfast in the house and a chicken coop to build."

"Oh...kay." Jerry reaches up to pat his matted hair down. He doesn't have a comb yet. He's going to build something. The anticipation has his heart racing.

His hands shake.

Farmer Blaine notices this. He raises an eyebrow observing Jerry's giddiness. "You okay, boy?" Jerry quickly puts his hands behind his back. He gazes at the ground afraid to look the farmer in the eye.

He nods. "Yes...I...I look forward to building something."

Farmer Blaine slaps Jerry in the back. "Good to hear, cause I can't do it m'self. First, let's go eat. I am one hungry man!"

Jerry builds the nerve to look Farmer Blaine in the eyes. He smiles meekly. "Me too."

*

In front of Jerry is a huge old farm table filled to the brim with bread, fried eggs, potatoes, biscuits, sausage gravy, grits, collard greens, bacon, pancakes, ham, fruit, orange juice, sweet tea, and milk. Jerry is very hungry, and the sight and warm inviting scent causes him to drool.

Farmer Blaine pulls out a chair at the table for Jerry.

"My boy, breakfast is the most important meal of the day. Eat up."

Jerry is thoroughly enjoying his new life. He never ate food so good.

"Maria comes in every morning to cook this up for us, bless her heart."

"Us?"

"Oh," Farmer Blaine chuckles, "I don't run this big ol' farm myself. I got migrants who come in and tend to the crops. They'll be here soon. Hell, you thought just you and I could eat all of this?" He laughs.

"I was...gonna...try," Jerry's talking with a mouthful of food.

Rumbling of trucks outside cuts into the conversation. He runs to a window. Three stake trucks roll to a stop. Each truck is loaded with eight to ten workers in the back. They pile out and head toward the house. Jerry backs into a corner. The men look different and speak a strange language. Ma always said all foreigners are terrorists. Terrorists do bad things.

Farmer Blaine waves him back to the table with a fork still in his hand. "What's wrong with you, boy? Nothin' to be afraid of here."

"*Que' hay para desayunar? Tengo hambre!*" The first man yells rubbing his stomach while entering the farmhouse.

Before you could say, "Bacon and eggs," the workers are at the table wolfing down the food.

"This here is Jerry," Farmer Blaine waves toward Jerry still in the corner.

"Hi, Jerry!" the men call out in unison.

Jerry waves. He studies the men looking for any weapons they may be holding. He doesn't see anything. The men don't seem as evil and threatening as Ma described either.

Farmer Blaine walks toward the door waving to Jerry to follow him. "Come on, we gotta lotta work to do."

Jerry follows at his heels. "Did...you hear...any...anything...weird last...night?" He figures if it's something that could hurt someone or one of the animals, the Farmer needs to know.

"Like what?" Farmer Blaine walks next to Jerry toward the old chicken coup across the drive from the farmhouse. He likes the chickens close so it's easy to get eggs in the morning.

"Like...a...scream?"

"A scream?"

Jerry nods.

"A scream like, aaaah?"

Jerry shakes his head, no. "More...like a...cat...fight...only real...real...loud."

Farmer Blaine chuckles, "Nope, never heard anything like that. I've got lots of animals here, cats too. Maybe the night air made them sound louder."

"May...be," Jerry nods.

Chapter 25

The Sacrifice

When Farmer Blaine and Jerry finish remodeling the chicken coop it looks more like a fortress. Jerry's proud of how hard he worked and how closely he'd followed Farmer Blaine's instructions. Hurricane winds won't be able to move it. The door is reinforced steel with a heavy gage latch that secures with a lock. Jerry wonders why they need a huge sliding bolt inside, but no questions, he remembers. Hardware cloth covers all openings and crevices of the coop. It also surrounds the chicken run. They install a rock perimeter to stop digging predators. They step back to admire their work. Jerry stands tall.

Farmer Blaine gathers his tools, "Your job, Jerry, is to close those doors every night and lock them."

Jerry nods.

"Gotta keep wild animals out."

"Like...what?"

"Like bears, coyotes, and hell, I'm sure there may be a bobcat out there. Maybe that's what made the noise you heard."

A rumbling in the distance signals to Jerry the migrant workers are heading home in their trucks. He considers his shack amid several empty ones lining the dirt road. "Why don't...they...stay here?" he points.

"Boy, I thought you don't ask questions," Farmer Blaine shoots back.

Jerry bows his head. "S...sorry."

"We got one more chore before we call it a night.

Let's go."

Farmer Blaine leads Jerry to the pig sty. Several pigs are milling about.

"Grab one of em."

Jerry stares at them. *Grab one? How?*

Farmer Blaine nods toward the sty. "Just get in there and do it." He points at a piglet in the corner. "That one. He's little. You can do it," He opens the gate for Jerry.

Jerry enters the muddy pen. The pigs calmly move out of his way. He tries to move slowly, but if he stands very long, he sinks into the soft, wet mud noisily sucking at his boots. He stealthily leans in to pick up a pig when it runs between Jerry's legs.

"Get it!" Farmer Blaine shouts.

Jerry stumbles in the mud, losing a boot somewhere in it. Pigs are running helter-skelter squealing in alarm. He corners the pig, dives for it, and falls face down in the mud. The pig squirms in his hands while Farmer Blaine cheers him on—the mud cold, wet, noxious. Jerry begins to lose his hold. He struggles to rise up to his knees. The pig has freed up all but one leg from Jerry's grip. Jerry holds onto that leg with a death grip while using his other hand to get free from the clutch of the muck.

"Squee...squeee...squeeee!" the pig's desperate cry rings in Jerry's ears. He's causing distress to a helpless creature. He wants to let go, but he must do what Farmer Blaine tells him. He rises to his feet and swings the pig into his arms, cradling it. The pig calms almost immediately.

"Look at you," Farmer Blaine chuckles. "Best laugh I've had in years. You're gonna need hosed off BEFORE gettin' in the shower."

Jerry plods out of the pen. The pig is quiet and calm in his arms. The others have settled down. Farmer Blaine. hands on his hips, gazes at them in awe.

"Damn if you ain't the pig whisperer." Jerry stares quizzically at the farmer.

"It's a good thing...means you're good with animals," Farmer Blaine laughs.

Jerry smiles and follows Farmer Blaine to a post at the edge of the property. The farmer takes a rope and ties one end to the post, the other around the pig's neck. Jerry sets the pig down.

"Remember, no questions." Farmer Blaine pulls on the rope to be sure it's secure. "Now, let's get you hosed off. I got some Spam and beans you can take to your shack for dinner. Big day tomorrow. Gotta run into Rockwell. I need supplies and we'll get ya some groceries."

Jerry brightens. He paws at his muddy hair. "And a comb." *I hope we go to the golden arches.*

*

Jerry is awakened in the middle of the night by distant squeals.

It sounds like the pig I tied up. Something is wrong.

He throws on a pair of pants and steps out into the moonlit night. He is approaching the pig when he sees a large shadow lurking behind it. When his eyes adjust, it is some kind of animal. It's black with grey mixed into the fur. Its face is almost like a bear's, with a mouth full of huge, sharp teeth. Its ears are large and pointed, standing straight up. Its body is like a panther's, only a lot bigger than one he saw in a zoo one time when his mother was nicer. It has a long fluffy tail.

Jerry sees something else...someone. Jerry ducks out of sight and watches. The creature hunkers down and growls. The pig squeals in terror.

"It's me, sweet Grimalkin. There is nothing to fear. You know I won't hurt you."

Jerry recognizes the voice--Farmer Blaine.

The creature edges toward the pig, opens its toothy jaws and bites down, immediately crushing the pig's head. Jerry covers his mouth to silence a scream. The creature lifts its head and gazes at the farmer. Jerry can't help but stare at its glowing yellow eyes. He recognizes the animal from the news. His pa was right, it's the panther. Both the creature and Farmer Blaine regard each other for an eternal moment before Grimalkin easily breaks the rope and drags the dead pig into the dark underbrush. Jerry gasps at its ungodly shrill wail. Farmer Blaine spins around at the sound Jerry uttered and stares into the night. Jerry doesn't move a muscle until the man gives up and walks away.

He runs to his shack and blocks the door with a chair. Sleep doesn't come easily. The words, "Sweet Grimalkin" echo in Jerry's ears.

Chapter 26

The Trip to Rockwell

"No...questions. No...ques...questions," Jerry keeps saying to himself on his way to Farmer Blaine's truck for their trip to Rockwell, but he does have questions; a bunch of them. Why would Farmer Blaine want an animal like that on his farm? Is he going to catch victims for the panther? He is not a killer; he doesn't want to catch animals to be fed to that monster. Does he know about Grimalkin helping that murderer dispose of guys?

"Good morning!" Farmer Blaine calls to him.

"Time to get a move on. Gonna be a beautiful day."

"Yes," Jerry jumps into the passenger seat. They had already eaten breakfast with the migrant workers who are now in the fields hard at work. Farmer Blaine drives down the lane amid harvester trucks slowly working their way through the golden oats.

"We're headin' to the Farm and Garden feed store. They're good people. I bring them pork for their sausages and in return they give me all the feed I need and then some...good people. It's a two-and-a-half-hour drive, but they make it worth the trip."

Jerry smiles and nods, "May...be we...could...go to...the golden...arches?"

Farmer Blaine laughs. "Mc Donald's? Oh hell, yeah. I love those quarter pounders. That is a definite stop, my boy."

Jerry chuckles. His parents never made him laugh. Farmer Blaine makes him laugh a lot. He has never met anyone so nice...besides Mr. Hart at the store of course. He hopes Kayla and Sarah will be there.

"You get a good night's sleep yet?" Farmer Blaine waves out the window at a harvester.

Jerry shakes his head, no. *Don't ask questions...don't ask questions.*

"Yeah, the pigs were riled up last night—made a lot of noise. I went out to see what the ruckus was all about, but I didn't see anything. Probably one of the sows in heat." Farmer Blaine raises an eyebrow glancing at Jerry.

Jerry shrugs, "It's been...pretty...hot...lately." *He's lying to me. Don't ask questions. Don't ask questions.*

Farmer Blaine chortles at Jerry's response. "Sure, boy, sure. Sounds to me I might have to explain the facts of life to you."

"The...facts?"

"The facts."

Jerry remembers his mother telling him the facts of life and how horrible it was giving birth to him.

He doesn't want to hear it again.

"It's...okay...I...I know," Jerry answers.

"Ya do? Well, good. There's better stuff to talk about during this trip...right?"

"Yeah." *Like why were you feeding the panther last night?*

"Those pigs get plenty loud when they're feelin' randy," Farmer Blaine chuckles.

Jerry laughs too, but it's stilted and fake.

"You okay? Got somethin' on your mind?" *No ques-tions...* "No...just...hungry."

"Hell, you just ate. Hmm, I'm thinkin' there's more to it than just a burger."

Jerry smiles sheepishly. "There...there's a girl...who...works there...I..."

"Oh ho! I thought so. Well, shoot, boy. Talk about feelin' randy." Farmer Blaine slaps his knees and shakes his head.

Jerry laughs—a real laugh. He has no idea who Randy is, but he sure isn't going to talk about feeling him.

*

After their business at the feed store Jerry and

Farmer Blaine go to McDonald's. While Blaine orders their lunch, Jerry scans the restaurant hoping to see Kayla when he is grabbed from behind by the shoulders.

"Jerry!" yells Kayla. "It's you!"

He turns to face Kayla, her sparkling eyes and soft brown hair captivating. He feels dizzy for a second.

"Hi." Jerry swallows.

"It's so good to see you. Sarah and I have been hoping things are going well for you."

Jerry nods. He feels sweaty in the air conditioning.

"Do you like working on a farm?"

Jerry nods, then hesitates. *How does she know I'm at a farm?* "How do...you...?"

"Have you been to the beach yet?"

Jerry shakes his head, *no*, having lost his train of thought.

"Food's here," Farmer Blaine strolls between the two and sets the food on a table. Jerry walks over followed by

Kayla. Sarah is busy at the register and signals to Kayla for help. Kayla raises her index finger, *in a minute.*

The two men sit down and begin unwrapping their burgers. Kayla continues.

"I was thinking like, on a day off Sarah, Nicky and I could come and pick you up and we could all go to the beach together...I mean, I haven't been to the beach in like forever, and I think it would be fun if you came along. We could swim and camp out and play beach volleyball and stuff." She takes a breath smiling wide. "What do you think?"

Farmer Blaine considers Kayla with one eye while the other is closed. His lips scrunch to one side reminding her of what she looks like when she puts on eyeliner. "Is this the girl you were hoping to see?"

Jerry stops in mid-bite and blushes. Kayla smiles warmly at him. Her eyes sparkle in the sunlight filtering through the restaurant windows. He quickly swallows what's in his mouth. "Oh...this...is Kayla."

"Hi," Kayla waves to Farmer Blaine.

"Kayla...this is...Mr..."

"Call me Blaine. I heard what you were askin'.

You are more than welcome to come by." He turns to Jerry. "Boy, do you realize this dish is asking you for a date?"

Jerry stares at Kayla, eyes wide—stupefied.

Kayla giggles, "Well, I...I wouldn't call it a date.

I just thought..."

"Yes!" Jerry blurts. "I...want to go to...the...ocean. Yes!"

"Slow down there, boy. I didn't say you have the time off to go," Farmer Blaine wipes ketchup from his mouth with a napkin.

"But..." Jerry's glee quickly disappears.

Farmer Blaine pulls a pen from his shirt pocket and jots a phone number on a clean napkin. "Here's Jerry's number. Call him when you're ready to come. We'll work something out," he winks, and hands Kayla the napkin.

Smiling, Kayla folds it and tucks it in her pocket.

"Thank you. See you later, Jerry." Kayla waves, heading back to work.

"You got yourself a real cutie there." Farmer Blaine winks.

Heat radiates from Jerry's face. He takes a big bite of burger.

"Some social worker out of the blue called me about hiring you. I think your little lady had something to do with it. Good with me, 'cause I really needed the help."

Jerry beams at Kayla talking animatedly to Sarah. *Do I have a girlfriend?*

Chapter 27

Kayla Calls

Jerry's job is building, securing, and cleaning pens for the animals during the day and tying a hog or a goat to the post weekly. Grimalkin, always there to get her meal—Farmer Blaine waiting to greet her. Sometimes she stays long enough for Farmer Blaine to pet her, other times she quickly steals into the night with her sacrifice. Jerry hates that part of the job, but he won't quit. His life now is many times better than when he lived with Ma and Pa. Sacrificing an animal once a week is his payment for this life.

One morning, at breakfast, knowing he can't ask the farmer, Jerry asks the crew if they know anything about the creature.

"*Aye, Grimalkin. Ten quedate lejos. Si no ella te come vivo...con dientes grandes y afilados!*" One of the men yells out.

"What?"

"Her name is Grimalkin. Stay away, or she will eat you with her big sharp teeth," one of the other men answers. "You are brave to live here."

"But why is...Farmer..." Jerry begins, but the men stand up from the table and leave him...alone.

No questions, Jerry slumps into his seat at the table. His cell phone rings. Word about his questions probably already got to Farmer Blaine and now Jerry's fired. In dread, he flips his phone open and answers, "Hello?" "Hi, Jerry, it's me...Kayla."

His breathing quickens. "Oh, hi," Jerry tries to be nonchalant—instead he sounds like he's been running for miles.

"Is this a bad time?"

"No! I...mean...heh, heh...no."

"We got this weekend off and thought we'd pick you up on the way to the beach. What do you think?"

"Yes! I...mean...I got...to clear...it...with...with..."

"Your boss, of course. Let me know what he says. We plan to be there Saturday about noon. We're gonna spend the night on the beach, so be sure to tell him you won't be back till sometime Sunday, okay?"

"O...kay."

"Kay, see ya then."

She hangs up before Jerry can say anything else. He hears music in his head. When his mother was in a good mood she would reminisce about the ocean and put her Beach Boys album on the record player. She would dance to the song, *and she'll have fun, fun, fun till her daddy takes her T-bird away*. It's Jerry's favorite memory of her. He wonders what kind of car Kayla will ride. He dances in the kitchen. Farmer Blaine walks in the door during mid-shuffle.

"What in tarnation?" Farmer Blaine throws his hands up in the air laughing.

Jerry stops. "I'm...going...to the...beach."

"Oh yeah? How so?"

"K...Kayla and...her friends...They..."

"Oh ho! Your little girlfriend, aye? When?"

"Sat...urday.   I'll   come   back...Sun...Sunday...if...it is...okay...with...you in all."

"Hmm," Farmer Blaine rubs his chin in thought.

"The pens are pretty secure, but what about Grimalkin's feeding?"

Jerry is shocked to hear Farmer Blaine say it. His mind is racing with questions he knows he can't ask.

Farmer Blaine continues, "I seen you lurkin' in the shadows at feeding time. I'll tell you this, I've cared for her for over twenty years. It all began in the winter of fifty-four. I found my dog in the yard. He was a big dog—almost ninety pounds and every ounce of blood was drained from him. I didn't know what to think.

Then, I heard more reports of dead animals...dogs, pigs, goats, chickens...folks were gettin' scared. "Our neighbor, Carl Pate said he saw the creature. Said it was five feet long, weighed about two-hundred pounds with a long bushy tail. Its eyes glowed yellow above a mouthful of sharp teeth—looked like a mix between a bear and a panther. It let out a high-pitched cry, like a baby wailin'. Its fur so dark, it was a shadow moving in the night. Carl said he saw a little one running beside it. Like maybe its youngin'.

"It got crazy. Hundreds of men were showing up in town loaded for bear. We were on the news and in the newspaper. One woman said it tried to run up at her whilst she stood on her porch calling for her missing mutt. They called it, *The Beast of Bladenboro*. The mayor called off the hunt before anyone got shot. He claimed a bobcat some guys shot and killed was the beast.

"The killings stopped for almost twenty years. My pa died and I owned the farm then. That's when I lost three pigs and two chickens. There wasn't a drop of blood in all of the dead animals."

Farmer Blaine stops his story to see if Jerry understands him. Jerry gazes at the Farmer, his eyes wide. He has one hundred percent of Jerry's attention.

"I decided not to tell anyone about it. I got my gun and went searching for it myself. I found prints by the pig sty. They were as large as the palm of my hand. Its talons had to be over an inch long—their prints extending beyond the paw. They didn't retract like a cat's would. I followed the prints into the forest. The path littered with broken branches led me to a huge old live-oak tree near a clearing. There was a large hollow opening at the base of it. I pulled out my flashlight, gun at ready and peered into the darkness. There she was, curled up in a ball, asleep. I was amazed my flashlight beam didn't wake her. A chewed pig's ear lay nearby. The creature looked just like the one Carl described, but there was something else...bones, some kind of remains of something next to it. They were huge. The animal's paws were awkwardly large. Her fur pitch black with a long fluffy tail wrapped around her like a soft blanket. She was very thin.

"I realized right then I was lookin' at the progeny of the beast. The remains she was lying beside were her mother. I heard a motor-like sound comin' from the creature. She was purring."

"Like a cat?" Jerry asks, but then, remembers, *no questions.*

"She opened her yellow eyes and gazed at me. I froze. She blinked. I saw God's creature in her face...innocence.

I could see that she wasn't part bear, only that her head was exceptionally large for a panther. She yawned—her razor-sharp teeth glowing in the beam of my flashlight. Amazingly she closed her eyes, and her motor began again. I made a hasty, quiet escape right then.

"I didn't know if anyone else lost livestock, but I knew I had to do something to prevent this one from running amok and killing like her mother did. So, I put out a sacrifice of a pig or goat every week to hold the creature off. It worked. First time I did it, I tied a small sixty-pound pig to a post outside of the sty. Late that same evening, I heard it squeal. I looked out to see the dark outline of the creature, her yellow eyes gleaming in the moonlight. She bit down on the pig's head, snapped the rope and drug it into the forest. I didn't breathe the whole time I watched.'

'Some months later, I got brave enough to follow her. She went into the same hollow tree I saw her before, but there was something else. She fed part of the pig to a kit. I don't know how it happened, that girl had mated somehow. The kit looked just like her. After a while, too many of my animals were disappearing and I had to do something about it. I built a cage and lured mama cat into it. She didn't like it one bit, no sir. At least my animals were safe. The kit only took what I tied on the post. The workers weren't happy with two panthers on the property, so they moved out. I'm grateful they stay to help harvest."

Farmer Blaine stops his story. His posture slumping and he spit on the ground. "Then, the worst happened. Somehow poachers found out about my cats and went hunting. They took the mama. I was out in the field when Grimalkin fled past me, the poachers in hot pursuit."

"Grim...al...kin?"

"Mean old puss." Farmer Blaine sucks at his teeth and smiles wryly.

"That's...what my...pa called..." Jerry hesitates. The lump in his throat prevents him from saying anything more about his parents. "I know...about...Gri...Grim..."

"I know too. I watch the news."

"It was...Kayla's...mother." The lump grows larger in Jerry's throat. Farmer Blaine may not allow her to come now.

"That's why we can't tell anyone about Grimalkin. Kayla's just picking you up. If you two start dating, she can't stay at our place."

For some reason, Jerry feels like he could throw up. Maybe it's the thought of actually dating. "I understand."

"How you gonna feed my cat Saturday night? I'm too old to chase down critters for her."

"I'll...tie one...up...before I...I go."

"Huh, I guess that'll work. You'll be back by Sunday night?"

Jerry nods.

"Alright then, I guess that'll work."

The lump is Jerry's throat is gone and he jumps up and down with glee. He's never been happier. He has a job, a home, and now, maybe a girlfriend...AND he's going to the beach. He shakes Farmer Blaine's hand enthusiastically.

"Woah there, boy. Don't rip my arm off," Farmer Blaine laughs rubbing his arm.

"I...am just...happy!" Jerry raises his arms in the air. "Whoop!"

Farmer Blaine chuckles at Jerry's earnestness. "Go ahead and call her back but, calm the heck down. We got work to do before Saturday." He waves both arms at Jerry to chill.

Jerry pulls his flip-phone from his front pocket. He opens it and stares at it. He has no idea how to call Kayla back. Farmer Blaine shakes his head, sighs deeply and takes the phone from Jerry. He's in no mood to explain how to use it all over again. He taps on it, then, hands it to Jerry. A ring tone chimes in his ear, then a click. Jerry's mouth forms a big "O" hearing Kayla's voice say, "Hello?"

"Hello?" he speaks into his phone.

"Yes...okay...yes...good...bye," Jerry closes his flip phone.

"All set?" Farmer Blaine asks.

Jerry nods.

"Then, let's get back to work."

Jerry fantasizes about Kayla and his big date as he cleans out the chicken coop. In his mind, Kayla is driving a classic Thunderbird convertible--her soft brown hair licking at her luscious lips in the breeze. He gets in the passenger seat, and she gives him a passionate kiss, like the ones he saw on his mother's soap operas.

The two of them are lying on a blanket on the beach as the sun sets. Kayla tells him she's falling in love with him. She rolls over and kisses him.

He jerks back to reality among a flurry of feathers. The chickens are in a panic. Jerry scans the coop and sees nothing...until he feels something slide across his boot. A big black snake. He freezes, afraid that if he moves, he'll get bit.

"Help," he begins softly. "Hel...p," louder. The snake continues his business slithering toward the nests filled with eggs. "Help...Helllp!"

A migrant worker bursts in. He grabs the shovel raising it high over his head. He slams the blade down to the back of the snake's head, cutting it off. The snake's body writhes headless. Jerry screams.

The worker laughs picking up the snake. "Scared?" he says with a heavy Spanish accent. "Rat snake. He just eat chickens," he laughs. "He not bite your hairy butt cheeks."

Jerry, finally able to relax, "Ha...ha...you are...so funny."

"Don't worry, I won't tell Mr. Blaine you left coop door open." He hands the shovel back to Jerry.

Jerry holds the shovel. The heat of embarrassment burns his cheeks and forehead.

*

Friday afternoon, the day before Jerry's big date, Farmer Blaine is checking on his tobacco crop growing on the east side of his lane. He runs a leaf between his fingers. The tobacco is ready for harvest. He begins to walk toward the barn for his tractor when he feels a sudden heaviness to his chest. He stops what he is doing waiting for the feeling to pass. It's happened to him before—probably the spicy Mexican dish he ate at supper. The feeling doesn't abate. It only gets worse, like his harvester is sitting on his chest. His jaw and left arm are tingling. He can't catch his breath. Farmer Blaine collapses reaching for the phone in his pocket.

Jerry dutifully ties a goat to the post for Grimalkin's dinner then, goes into his shack. He doesn't want the image of the beast eating that poor goat to tarnish his fantasy of seeing Kayla. He hears the plaintive bleat of the goat as Grimalkin creeps near. He turns on the TV cranking up the sound, but it doesn't drown out the piercing wail from Grimalkin. It's not its usual shrill call...it's more like a cry of alarm.

Something is wrong with her. Jerry rushes out the door and stops several feet from the feeding post. The goat and Grimalkin are gone. So is Farmer Blaine. He is always there for her feedings. Jerry flips open his phone and taps buttons. He can't remember which ones to tap, and he doesn't hear anything. In fact, the screen of his phone is black. Nothing. He tosses his dead phone back into his pocket and runs to the farmhouse. He bangs on the door. No answer. He tries the door handle...locked. He can't even go through a window. Farmer Blaine had installed bars on them.

"Farmer Blaine! You...in...there?

Hey...Farmer...Mr... Springer!"

A growl echoes. Jerry can't tell which direction it's coming from when an earsplitting howl consumes the air around him.

He bolts for his shack, running for his life. The padded thud of paws hit the ground behind him, a huff with every step. He crashes onto his door turning the knob at the same time and falls into his shack. He jumps up and slams the door. The creature bashes against it. Jerry holds it shut, pushing with all of his might. He slides the bolt of the lock into place. A loud *rush-brrr*, like a bottle rocket. Silence.

Chapter 28

A Turn of Events

Beams of sunlight shoot through his front window warming the floor at Jerry's feet. He had only a few hours of sleep after sitting on his couch guarding the door all night. It had been quiet...too quiet. He put the cast-iron skillet he was holding in his lap back in its place in the kitchen and shakes the night's events from his mind like waving through cobwebs. The night is over. Jerry is happy it's a new day. *Today is the day I'm going to the beach.*

First, Jerry needs to find Farmer Blaine. The migrant farm crew rumbles up the lane in their trucks. Inside

Farmer Blaine's home, breakfast is being prepared same as always.

Jerry approaches the cook, Maria. "Have...you seen...Farmer...B..."

She shakes her head. "I have a key. Sometimes he check fields before he eats."

"Thank...you." Jerry's a bit hopeful. *Maybe Farmer Blaine sleeps really hard. I hope Maria is right. I hope he's back before Kayla gets here.*

After breakfast, the crew heads out to harvest the to-bacco. Jerry is to put fresh straw in the pig sty, but he's too preoccupied with thoughts of going to the beach with

Kayla and wondering where Farmer Blaine is. He sits on the straw pondering.

*

Kayla runs out of the house with her backpack loaded with her swimsuit, towels, snacks, and a myriad of supplies toward Nick's blue 2007 PT Cruiser. The pack making her look like a hunchback. Shep runs after her almost tripping her. He jumps into the open car door ahead of her.

"No, Shep. You can't go with us today," Kayla pulls on his collar to get him to move. The dog whines attempting to hold his ground.

"Shep...come," demands Uncle Mike. The dog bows his head and obediently exits the car whining the whole time.

Sarah opens the back window. "You sure Shep can't come along?"

"No, I don't want to worry about keeping him on a leash at the beach. He'll be fine," Kayla waves to Shep and Mike.

"Be safe," Mike calls out to them.

Kayla lugs her backpack onto the rear seat. She leans out of Nick's car window. "We will, Uncle Mike. Love you!"

Shep continues to whine and pace. He is not happy about the situation at all. He barks at the departing auto. Mike gives him a reassuring pat.

As Nick drives, Kayla, and Sarah gab animatedly over the noise of the radio.

"I brought baby oil. I need a tan. Sunscreen just doesn't do it. I mean, I got like one day to get one going," Sarah pulls baby oil out of her beach bag and shows it to Kayla.

"You'll burn."

"So? It'll turn into a tan. It always does."

"Or your skin will peel," Nick chimes in.

"Oh, Gawd, no. I never do. I just slather on lots of aloe afterwards...it works."

"So, you say. I'm using SPF thirty. I'm not taking any chances." Kayla leans forward from the back seat. "Nicky, thanks for doing this for us."

"No problem. I like road trips. I thought Shep would come with us."

"Why?"

"You know, to protect you from strangers. You don't really know Jerry. He could be a rapist or something."

Kayla scoffs, "Uncle Mike said the same thing. Shoot, I need more protection from you than poor Jerry. Shep has never been around farm animals before. He would probably freak out, not to mention watching him at the beach. It would've been too much work."

"I guess you're right," Nick shrugs. "I just feel so bad for Jerry. I mean, here's this guy who was a prisoner in his own home for fifteen years—rarely going outside. He has never seen the ocean."

"I heard his parents treated him like a dog. They deserved to rot where they sat," adds Sarah placing her oil back in the bag.

"Anyway," Kayla sighs, "I understand where he's coming from, and I want to help. You guys are the best for going along with me."

"Yeah, yeah." Sarah crosses her arms. "But don't make me his date...not going there."

Kayla laughs, "Duh, I know!"

A good song comes on the radio. Nick turns up the volume. "Life is a Highway", by Rascal Flatts is playing.

All of them sing, *"Life is a highway...I wanna ride it all night long. If you're going my way...I wanna drive it all night long..."*

*

Jerry's preoccupation is interrupted by a loud, piercing scream. The farm hands are running through the tobacco field like children running from their mother holding a whip. Two of them are carrying a body. A dark shadow gallops behind them, whisking the leaves of the plants blowing in a windstorm.

"Grim...alkin," Jerry whispers to himself.

The men drop the body running to jump onto the backs of the fleeing trucks. The beast stops at what the men dropped. Jerry stands statue still afraid any movement will attract Grimalkin's attention. She sniffs at the body. She paws at it.

Jerry's heart drops to his gut. *What if it's Farmer Blaine?*

Grimalkin keens to the sky a baleful sonic cry, her teeth glistening in the sun. Jerry covers his ears with both hands. She drops out of sight—a shadow moving through the field.

Jerry rushes to the chicken coop, dumps the chicken feces out of the wheelbarrow and runs with it toward the body, all the while scanning the area for the creature.

He stops--recognizing the body. "Farmer...Blaine!" Jerry runs to him and pats him. There is no response.

Farmer Blaine's eyes have the blank lifeless stare his parents had when he let them go. "No!" he sobs, "Please, not...again...not again!" He falls onto the farmer.

The rustle of leaves. His eyes jerk around searching the field. Jerry jumps up and begins to put Farmer Blaine in the wheelbarrow. It's a struggle. A low guttural growl comes from behind.

He runs. Farmer Blaine is mostly in the wheelbarrow—his arms and legs flapping about as Jerry pushes the barrow through the stalks of tobacco heading for the nearest building, the chicken coop. He pulls open the door and shoves the wheelbarrow inside. He swears he feels hot breath on his neck. He slams the door. Jerry is slides the deadbolt into its sleeve. Grimalkin lets out a sickening high squeal. She bashes against the door. The chickens flip out--flying everywhere, flapping into Jerry and Farmer Blaine. A few die right on the spot. Feathers and chicken feces fill the air. Jerry coughs picking up a shovel. He covers his nose with his shirt.

Grimalkin continues to scream as she bashes onto the coop. Jerry stands in a corner holding the shovel in front of him for protection.

Silence--no bashing or wailing. The chickens calm down and settle onto their roosts.

Oh no, Kayla is coming, Jerry remembers. He reaches into his pocket for his cell phone. He flips it open. He has forgotten his phone is dead. Jerry throws it against a wall in total frustration and puts his face into the palms of his hands. After a moment, he realizes Farmer Blaine will have his phone. He gingerly feels the pockets of Farmer Blaine's pants. He finds a wallet, but no phone. It must have been dropped somewhere.

"Argh!"

A motor. Jerry jumps up on a roosting bar peering out a gap near the ceiling. A car is pulling up to Farmer Blaine's house. Beautiful Kayla steps out along with Sarah. There's a guy with them. They're talking happily stepping onto the porch. A low growl is emanating from outside of the coop. He can't see it. Panic sets in.

"Run!"

The group turns in search of who is yelling when they see Grimalkin running toward them. Nick opens the door of the farmhouse. The three rush inside. Grimalkin mounts the porch.

Jerry watches the beast lean against the door and scratch at it, the girls screaming inside. He's helpless to save them, but relieved Maria didn't lock the door after breakfast.

Grimalkin lurches to a window of the house and bashes it in. The screaming continues. She paws through the bars and gnashes her teeth at them. She jerks a paw away and yelps. Jerry sees blood on it. She has cut herself on broken glass. Grimalkin flees into the woods.

*

"Oh, my Gawd! What was that? What was it?" Sarah cries.

"What do we do? What do we do? Oh, God...oh, God," Kayla screams.

"Shhh! Listen," Nick yells. Everyone becomes silent.

"Hello?" Jerry calls out.

Kayla runs to the window. "Jerry? Jerry, is that you?"

"Yeah!"

"Was that...?"

"Grim...alkin!"

Kayla can't believe her ears. How did the panther end up here? How did he know her name is Grimalkin?

"How did she end up here? How did you know her name?"

"Farmer...Blaine! She's his...pet...he named...her, but...she's not...nice!"

"We know! She..." Kayla stops herself and wonders if she is having some kind of weird nightmare. This is a bad situation.

Chapter 29

Trapped

"What do we do?" Memories of almost touching the beast latches to Kayla's mind.

"I...don't...know!" Jerry calls out from the chicken coop.

"I know." Nick bends down to tie his shoe. "We get outta here."

"But, what about Jerry?"

"Tell him we'll count to three and everyone run for the car," Nick stretches.

"Jerry," Kayla yells out the window. "When I count to three, run to the car...got it?"

"Farmer...Blaine...is in...here. He can't...run."

"He's in there with you?" She's hopeful Mr. Springer knows a way out.

"Yeah...but...he's not...moving. I...think he's...hurt."

Kayla's hand covers her mouth.

Nick runs to the window. "We'll come back for him later!"

"But what if we leave him and Grimalkin eats him?" Kayla grabs Nick's shirt.

"We can't worry about that now. We gotta get ourselves outta here," Nick whispers harshly at her.

"O...kay!" Jerry must leave Farmer Blaine behind in the chicken coop and he won't have time to lock the door.

"One!"

This is not how it should end for Farmer Blaine.

"Two!"

She'll eat all the chickens.

"Thr..." Grimalkin comes out of nowhere and jumps on Nick's PT Cruiser. The driver's window shatters. She jumps down and leaps into the now open car. The Cruiser rocks as Grimalkin tears into the cushions of the seats. She backs into the steering-wheel causing the horn to blow. Startled, she springs out of the car and bites the wheels. The girls scream amid the hiss of escaping air. The creature head butts the front of the car. Fluid from the radiator spills out. The car is history.

"Shit, shit, shit!" Nick pounds the window sill with his fist.

"Now what do we do?" Sarah is weeping tightly gripping Kayla.

"Let me try," Kayla pulls her phone from her back pocket. She taps...

"Nine, one, one," a pleasant voice over the phone.

"What is (static) emergency?"

"Help! A panther just ruined our car and we're trapped! We're on Route two-eleven west of town. It's a big farm...hello...hello? Crap, I lost them!"

"Shit!" Nick tries his phone. "It must be the house. I bet I can get reception outside."

"No, no, no! She's out there. You'll be killed," Kayla cries.

"Maybe they got the message. They'll be here soon," Sarah releases Kayla.

"Maybe," agrees Kayla. "Let's wait and see."

Nick puts his phone back in his pocket and paces. He goes to the kitchen and finds water, juice, and food in the refrigerator. "At least we have something to eat and drink while we wait."

"I can't even think about food right now." Sarah nods in agreement.

After waiting two hours in silence no help has arrived. Kayla pulls her phone out of her pocket and looks. It's dead.

"Crap!"

"What?"

"My phone's dead."

"Did you remember your charger?"

"Yeah, it's in my backpack...which is in the car."

"Shit."

Kayla paces, "I don't think they're coming."

"What about Jerry?" Sarah asks. "He lives here. He must know a way to help us."

Kayla's eyes grow wide. In her wait for the police, she has forgotten about Jerry. "Jerry!" She runs to the broken window. "Jerry!"

It is hot inside the chicken coop. Jerry is sweating through his shirt. His worst fear is coming true. Farmer Blaine is beginning to smell rancid, just like his mother did when she died. The chickens mill about uneasily. He hears Kayla's sweet voice. He jumps up and shouts through the gap near the ceiling, "Kayla?"

"Do you have any food or water?"

"No!"

Nick pushes Kayla aside. "You have any idea how to get us out of here?" Jerry thinks hard.

"Well?"

"No."

"What about a car or truck? Isn't there one around here somewhere?"

"He...has a...truck."

"Great! Where?"

"In...the car...barn."

"Where's the car barn?"

"In...the barn!"

Nick gapes out the window. The barn is at the end of the lane, past the chicken coop. It has to be at least a half mile away.

"Son of a...!" Nick paces again. He runs upstairs.

"Can you get to the house?" Kayla calls out to Jerry.

Jerry scans what he can see from the chicken coop. He swears he can hear Grimalkin breathing, huffing, and growling. The chickens are restless.

"No," he responds.

Nick runs down the stairs with a shotgun in his hands. "I found it in one of the bedrooms. I found bullets too." He opens a hand to reveal several shotgun shells. He loads the gun and nods to Kayla.

"Jerry, run to the house. Nick will cover you."

Sarah points at her head meaning Jerry won't under-stand.

"Oh, Nick will shoot it if it comes after you."

Shoot her? Jerry thinks. *Shoot Grimalkin? Farmer Blaine loved her. What to do?* He begins to slide the deadbolt. Its click coming out of the sleeve alerts Grimalkin which stirs the chickens.

Grimalkin wails. Feathers fly. Jerry quickly replaces the bolt. The beast slams herself against the coop. Dust and dander fills the air. Jerry coughs, bracing himself against a wall.

The beast slams against the coop, her crazed yellow eyes, her body twice the size of any bear or cat. Her movements fast as a rattlesnake's strike. Nick aims the gun.

"She's too far away!"

"I'll call her." Sarah rushes to the window and stands next to Nick. "Here, kitty, kitty, kitty."

"What are you doing?" Nick shouts when Grimalkin disappears into the tobacco field.

Silence. The chickens calm down.

"I was trying to get it to come so you can shoot it." Sarah blinks innocently.

"That thing would have had your throat before I even had the chance."

"Oh."

Kayla enters the room with two bottles of water in one hand and food in a baggy in another. "I'm taking this to Jerry while Grimalkin is gone."

"You crazy?" Sarah blocks the door, arms outstretched.

"I'm a good runner and Nick will cover me." Kayla tucks the bag under one arm.

"Oh, my Gawd, I can't believe you're gonna do it."
"It'll be okay—I'm fast."

Sarah edges away from the door. "If Shep was here he would chase that cat away."

"Seriously?" Kayla places her free hand on her hip. "That cat would eat my dog. Stop worrying, you're making me nervous."

Kayla unlocks the door followed by Sarah to lock it again when she's out. Nick moves to the window with the shotgun pointing it at the coop. Kayla tip toes across the porch and down the steps. Leaves rustling in the field—Grimalkin emerges. Kayla darts for the coop forty yards away, the cat hot on her heals. Nick shoots and misses. A tug on Kayla's leg almost causes her to fall. Righting herself, she leaps toward the door of the chicken coop. Jerry quickly pulls on the bolt, opens the door while pulling her inside at the same time pushing the door shut and bolting it. Grimalkin wails. The chickens flutter. Kayla touches something hot and wet on her thigh.

She holds up her bag filled with bottles of water and food. "I...brought you...this," she pants.

"You're...hurt," Jerry rushes to her side.

She examines her thigh. It's a deep cut—one that could use some stitches. "Oh!"

Jerry stares at the wound, "It's my...fault. I let...you...get...get hurt."

"You didn't let me get hurt. I just didn't run fast enough," Kayla says. "Hey, I made it, didn't I?" Jerry nods.

She gingerly touches her injury and flinches, "I need something for this."

Jerry gawks.

"Give me your shirt."

He takes off his shirt as Kayla hands him her bag. She tears a strip of cloth from the shirt and ties it to her thigh.

"I'm...sorry...Kayla..."

"You'll be sorry if after risking my life to get over here, you don't eat what's in that bag." She reaches into her sack and brings out a bottle of water. "I even brought extra in case you ask me to stay."

Jerry stares blankly. "Why would I...ask you...to stay in a...chicken...coop?"

"I'm kidding...just trying to lighten things up around here." Kayla hands Jerry the water and gazes around the chicken coop. When her eyes land on Farmer Blaine she raises the back of her hand to cover her nose.

Jerry takes a long swig of water. His posture slumps. Tears well in his eyes. "I...think he's...dead."

"Oh, Jerry...I'm sorry." She eases toward Farmer Blaine. He has lost all of the color in his skin except for blotchy red patches where his blood has settled. His body has released fluid and he is beginning to swell.

"Is...he...dead?"

Kayla regards Jerry sadly. He's so hopeful and she must tell him, "He's been dead awhile...maybe for a few days?"

Jerry sobs. "I...found him...in...the field. The...workers...the workers...were... taking him...away."

Kayla moves closer to the cadaver to get a better look. "I don't see any injuries."

"Grim...Grimalkin...didn't kill...him?" Jerry sniffs and wipes his nose on the crook of his arm.

"I don't think so."

Jerry, overwhelmed, bends over sobbing in relief the farmer didn't die violently. "Farmer...Blaine...was my...friend. He...helped...me..."

Kayla approaches Jerry and lifts his head to meet hers. She embraces him in her arms. He weeps into her shoulder. Jerry doesn't understand why his loved ones have left him. Their bodies rot away as if they never existed at all.

*

Grimalkin is pacing around the outside of the chicken coop. Nick attempts to take aim at it with the shotgun.

"Shit, she's too far away."

"Isn't there something with a higher caliber around here?" Sarah asks as she finishes a bottle of water.

"I'll look around again." Nick ascends the stairway. Sarah gazes out of the window and watches Grimalkin pace. The sun is setting. "You really are the offspring of the *Beast of Bladenboro*...amazing." She walks into the kitchen, takes bologna and bread from the refrigerator, and begins to make a sandwich. "It's gonna be a long night."

Nick comes down the stairs still holding on to the shotgun. "No luck. I guess we're stuck here for the night.

Charge your phone and in the morning, I'll go out and call 911 when I get a signal."

"Out there?" Sarah points at the door with her sandwich. "What about...it?"

"Don't they hunt at night?"

"They? You ever see another one? You know that is no ordinary feline." Sarah slams her empty plate on the counter and stabs her forehead with her index finger.

"Think! It's Grimalkin. You know, the one that almost had you for dinner!" She rips a bite of her sandwich with her teeth, smacking her lips as she eats.

Nick waves her off and peers out the window. Grimalkin settles herself in front of the chicken coop curling into a ball. "Hey, maybe I can go out while she's sleeping."

"Wait a while." Sarah swallows her bite of bologna sandwich.

Chapter 30

The Long Night

Darkness falls, the chickens settle onto their roosts for the evening. The coop is dark inside. Jerry peeks out of the gap near the ceiling. Cooler air wafts over his face. He spies Grimalkin curled up asleep nearby.

"She's sleeping," he whispers to Kayla.

"I guess we're here for the night." Kayla can't see much in the dark, so she pulls a flashlight from her bag.

Jerry stares, mouth wide in surprise.

"I'm glad I found this," she smiles. "I was a Girl Scout once, you know? Always be prepared." She flicks the switch on the flashlight bathing the chicken coop floor in light.

Jerry's mouth continues to hang open in awe. "Can I...see...that?"

She hands the light to him. He locates the bales of fresh straw he had put in a corner this morning. The shovel leans against the wall beside it—a job he didn't finish. He hands the flashlight back to Kayla. She holds the beam in his direction while he uses the shovel to scrape chicken feces off of a section of the floor. He picks up the fresh straw and spreads it over the newly cleaned spot.

Kayla takes the remains of Jerry's shirt and covers her nose and mouth from the dust and stink. The perspiration odor left by Jerry onto his shirt is much better than the mixture of chicken poop and death.

When he finishes, he takes Kayla by the hand to help her sit on the fresh straw. The bleeding of her thigh has stopped, but now it's throbbing in pain.

She grimaces from the strain. "Thank you."

"Are...you...okay?"

"I'm fine. My scratch just aches a bit."

Jerry paces, unsure of what to do next.

"I'll be fine...really." Kayla pats the straw next to her. "Come...sit."

Jerry's heart races at the thought she wants him to sit next to her. He drops onto the straw next to her sitting Indian style--a huge smile plastered on his face.

She flicks off the flashlight. "We might need to save the batteries."

A sliver of moonlight glows through the gap near the ceiling of the chicken coop.

Kayla feels for Jerry's hand and holds it. His breathing quickens with his speeding heart. Tingling moves up his arm through his torso and down his legs. He sweats.

"I really feel bad calling the cops on you. I didn't know what had happened to you. I just thought you were...uh..." Kayla isn't sure she should go on. It may hurt Jerry's feelings.

"I...was...what?"

"Um...oh boy..." She adjusts herself gazing at the floor. "Like a dumb robber."

Jerry covers his mouth to contain explosive laughter. "I...am. I had...to give it...all...back." The tension leaves him in his glee.

Kayla laughs. Their laughter stirs the chickens, which could stir Grimalkin. They stop...and snicker quietly. She falls serious. "Jerry, I know all about Grimalkin. She hurt Nicky once. My mother...used her. I didn't realize I was sending you to deal with all of this." "Sending...me?"

"I...my friend, Sarah's mom, got you this job. I asked her to. I thought you would like to live on a farm...one closer to the beach," her grip tightens on Jerry's hand.

"I...do like...it here. Farmer...Blaine said...he took...care of Grim...Grimalkin...for a long...time.

How...would you...know...?"

"I didn't know. All I know is my mother used her to get rid of men she "accidently" killed. She named the panther Grimalkin too. I mean, how freaky is that?"

"Pa...saw it...on the...the news. She's in jail...now? How...did...how did she...use...?"

"She had Grimalkin drag them away and bury them in the woods. My mom gave her fresh meat for doing it. I had to stop her. She had her own brother trapped in the walk-in freezer. When I went up to her room, Grimalkin was there. The gun went off. I thought I shot her. This is all so crazy!"

Kayla is talking as fast as she did in McDonald's. All of this new information has Jerry's mind spinning into overload. "I...I..."

"Oh, Jerry." She takes his hand into both of hers. "I know what happened to you. My mother..." Kayla pauses to hold back the tears welling in her eyes. "My mother killed my father too."

Rolling his dead father under the basement stairs flashes in Jerry's mind. He tries to shake off the thought. "My mother forced me to help her," Kayla chokes back tears.

Jerry gasps, realizing Kayla had to endure horrors very similar to his—maybe worse. He rises to his knees, holds her gently in his arms and rocks her.

"Then, I found out that my uncle is my real father. I don't even know who my real mother is. I was adopted." Kayla sobs onto his bare chest. "And now my mom is in prison for...aggravated murder."

"I...I wish...," Jerry begins. He wishes he had met her in another life—a normal life where they could have met at a party or somewhere happy and they could be a couple. They have too much sadness in common...and now, Grimalkin.

"It's amazing that my mom *and* your farmer named her Grimalkin. You know?" Kayla feels safe in Jerry's arms. She hugs him fiercely. "You're a good man, Jerry. You deserve a good life. You need to get away from all of this...mess."

"I'm...happy...here...with you."

"Oh, Jerry," Kayla whispers, and kisses him on the cheek.

It's the happiest day of Jerry's life.

*

It's well after midnight. The farm is quiet—no movement, except in the living room. Nick prepares to go out of the door, slip past Grimalkin and call for help. He gently wraps his hand around the doorknob and turns. It is silent. He slowly pulls the door open. It makes a gentle *cree* sound. He freezes. There is no movement from the large hump in the yard where the slight aura of the moon indicates the shape of Grimalkin. Nick points the shotgun at her and tiptoes onto the porch. Step by step he creeps to the lawn, still no movement from the creature. He stealthily moves toward the driveway. Surely a signal will be there. Nick taps on his phone searching for a signal. The light emitting from the phone breaks open the night, alerting Grimalkin. Nick has a signal. The yellow glow of Grimalkin's eyes slices through the air toward him. He drops his phone and shoots.

Jerry awakens with a start. He is leaning against the wall with Kayla's head in his lap. His jerk wakes Kayla. Nick screams. Without even looking to see what is going on, Jerry grabs a chicken by its legs, unbolts the door and runs out.

"Hey!" he yells, waiving the chicken.

Nick is running toward the farmhouse with Grimalkin at his heals.

"Hey!" Jerry shouts again. Grimalkin stops to sniff the air and discharges a low reverberating growl.

Sarah opens the door. Nick falls in. She slams and bolts it.

Grimalkin is distracted by Jerry's actions. Kayla grabs the shovel, limping to the door, the blade at ready to strike should Jerry fall into trouble. The beast stalks toward Jerry—edging ever closer. When she is only feet from him, he throws the chicken at her. Grimalkin gives it a cursory glance and lunges toward Jerry.

"Get in...get in!" Kayla screams.

Jerry jumps back into the coop. Kayla tries to push the door shut, but Grimalkin is working her way in. Jerry shoulders the door. Kayla brings the blade of the shovel down on Grimalkin's leg. It doesn't seem to make a difference. The beast is pushing through, his muzzle full of teeth. The chickens flop against the walls of the coop in a search for escape. They fly into Jerry and Kayla. She screams amid the chaos and again swings down the blade of the shovel with all of her might cutting Grimalkin's leg. The creature yelps in pain and pulls away from the door. Jerry bolts it.

Grimalkin's shrieks of agony and anger pierce the air.

*

"Are you okay?" Sarah asks Nick. He rises from the floor and feels himself for any injuries. "Yeah, I'm fine...I think."

"Were you able to call?"

Nick spreads his hands open, realizing he dropped his phone. "No...shit. I dropped it. We'll have to wait till morning. I hope Jerry and Kayla are alright. I think they hurt it."

The familiar *rush-brrr* like a bottle rocket whenever Grimalkin is near...then, silence—not even the noise of the night crickets.

The chickens in the chicken coop mill about in an eerie hush. Jerry gets up on a roost and peers out the gap.

The chicken is still there...alive, no sign of Grimalkin.

Kayla flips on the flashlight and checks out the bandage on her leg. Blood has drenched the piece of shirt she wrapped on it. Jerry dismounts the roost. Kayla quickly switches it off. She doesn't want to alarm him.

Chapter 31

The Standoff

Nick is awake at the crack of dawn. He cups his hands to the sides of his face and leans against them to cut out any glare of the window to look for any sign of

Grimalkin—she's not out there. He unbolts the door and steps out onto the porch. The light of morning glints off of the screen of his cellphone lying in the grass nearby. "Hey!" he yells. "Where are you, you mangy old cat? A mix between a panther and a bear...why you're a Pear! Yeah, an old, dried-up pear!" Nick listens.

The chirps of birds greeting the morning are all he hears. He yells again, "You hungry? Huh? Hey!"

The tops of the trees sway in the breeze. It all could have been a nightmare, but his trashed car is proof that it wasn't. There is no sign of Grimalkin.

Nick's shouting awakens Jerry and Kayla. Jerry peeks out to see Nick strolling down the farmhouse steps and onto the driveway. He picks up his phone and stares down at it while walking the lane toward the tobacco field.

"Can we get out of here now?" Kayla struggles to get to her feet.

Her leg covered in dried blood. Jerry wants to pick her up and run out of there—instead, he shakes his head, no. His instinct tells him it's not time.

"But your farmer guy is beginning to really stink, and he's freaking me out, and it's hot in here, and my leg really hurts." Kayla pulls on Jerry's arm to help her up.

"Nick...is going...to call...9...1,1." He holds her up, but the pain in Kayla's leg is too much. She sits back down.

"There's no sign of Grimalkin?" Jerry shakes his head, no.

Nick finally gets a signal beside the tobacco field. The breeze gently blows the tops of the plants making them resemble ocean waves. He quickly taps the numbers, 9,1,1.

"This is nine, one, one, what is your emergency?" a pleasant female voice says on the other end.

"Help! We're trapped by a big animal at a farm north of Bladenboro. People are hurt!"

"What type of animal?"

"A panther...a big one. Please, just come, someone is hurt." Nick doesn't know for sure if anyone is hurt, but he knows it'll get help out faster.

"We'll send someone right away. What is your address?"

"It's a farm on route two-eleven near Butler Mill Road...like a half mile down. I...I don't know the house number." A path is mowing through the tobacco field-the fin of a shark cutting through the ocean. Nick's breath catches in his chest around his speeding heart. The charming voice on the other end, "Just stay on the line and we'll locate..." Nick runs. Grimalkin swipes at him, hitting his leg. He falls, dropping his phone. Nick flips to his back and attempts to crawl backward, his leg is cut to the bone.

Grimalkin creeps ever closer to him sniffing the air.

Her guttural growl vibrates in Nick's chest. Breathing is difficult at the horror of the gleam in Grimalkin's teeth amid the spots floating in front of his eyes. He loses consciousness.

*

The scene unfold before Jerry and realizes what he must do. He gathers his will, swallows hard and runs to the door of the coop.

"Lock the...d...door!" he races out toward the field.

Kayla tries to get to her feet, but her leg buckles underneath her. Pain sears up her injured leg. "Shit!" She sits holding her leg. Red streaks are running up her thigh indicating infection is setting in. "Now what do I do?" she calls over to Farmer Blaine knowing he can't answer her. He lies in the wheelbarrow swollen and oozing of stink. The chickens have grouped together in the opposite corner of the coop—feathers ruffled.

Jerry stands between Nick and Grimalkin. She rears up on her hind legs and growls, her hackles raised. Her teeth mere inches from Jerry's face. He grimaces. Words he heard Farmer Blaine say comes to his mind.

"My...sweet...Grimalk-in," doing his best to sound calm and sincere, when all he wants to do is scream and run.

His legs shake uncontrollably.

Grimalkin places a paw on Jerry's shoulder and sniffs his face, her ochre eyes staring into his. He prays she doesn't see fear. Nick lies unconscious behind him. Grimalkin's hackles lower— her fur smooths. Her muzzle covers her teeth giving her the sweeter appearance of a pussy cat. She nuzzles him on the other shoulder. She wants something.

Instinctively, Jerry reaches his hand out to scratch her behind an ear, knowing full well she could bite it off in an instant. Instead, she leans into his hand. A loud motor-like purr emerges from deep inside of her, the rumble coursing through his hand. Her fur is rough, like his mother's hair when he washed it for her. Maybe

Farmer Blaine is right. She is only doing what she's been made to do. She's the only one of her kind.

"Sweet...Grimalkin."

Grimalkin pulls away from him, turns and runs toward the chicken coop.

"Kayla!" Jerry moves to run, but he's got to stop

Nick's profusely bleeding leg. He prays Kayla bolted the door.

Jerry is shirtless, so he tears a strip of fabric from Nick's T-shirt and ties it above the wound to create a tourniquet. His mother did that once to Jerry's arm when he accidentally cut it chopping wood for the fireplace. She even stitched it up herself and told Jerry she didn't need no idiot doctor charging her an arm and a leg to do it. Nick's cut is way too big for him to fix...besides, Jerry's never done it before.

His thoughts flood back to Kayla. He looks up from Nick. Grimalkin swipes the door open and enters the coop.

"Kayla!" Jerry runs toward the coop.

Sarah darts out of the farmhouse toward Nick.

Grimalkin creeps into the chicken coop. Chickens squawk and flutter about—feathers and dander flying in and out of the sunbeam streaming through the gap near the ceiling. Kayla sits against the wall opposite the door. Her head is bowed. Grimalkin stalks toward her. Kayla doesn't move. *I wish Shep was here.* Grimalkin sniffs at her injured leg and licks it. The beast's tongue, like sandpaper, causes the pain in Kayla's leg to erupt once again.

She sucks in a gasp of air doing her best not to cry out. The creature jerks back at the noise and cocks her head to one side. She sniffs the air again and spies Farmer Blaine in the wheelbarrow.

Jerry's frantic calls outside grow louder. Grimalkin bites down on Farmer Blaine's leg and drags him out of the coop.

Grimalkin is dragging a body into the underbrush as Jerry approaches. He can't tell who it is. "Kayla!"

"Here. I'm in here."

Jerry dashes into the chicken coop. Kayla is alive. He falls onto his knees and holds her in his arms. Both shudder and sob.

"I couldn't bolt the door. I can't walk," Kayla cries.

Jerry rocks her. "It's...okay. I...got you." He stands and picks up Kayla in his arms.

She winces in anguish. "She took your farmer."

Jerry carries her out of the coop.

Chapter 32

Lost Love

Sarah runs into the tobacco field to where Nick lies. She shakes him.

"Nick. Nick. Are you alive? Please be alive. Please. God."

Nick awakens with a jerk...remembering Grimalkin's teeth, he flails about.

She holds him down, "Nick, it's me, Sarah."

"Sarah? Wha...?"

"They're on the way."

"Who?"

"The police...911. They got your call. By the time I called they're already on their way...listen."

Sirens in the distance are growing louder.

"You're going to be okay," Sarah smiles, petting Nick.

"Okay," Nick sounds like he awoke from a very deep sleep.

Jerry carries Kayla across the yard. Sarah waves two police cars and an ambulance onto the property to where Nick is lying. EMTs rush to Nick's aid. A policeman rushes over to help Jerry carry Kayla.

"What the hell happened here?" asks the officer.

Jerry's out of breath and doesn't answer.

Sarah runs over to them. "Kayla, are you okay? Oh, my Gawd...your leg!"

"I'll be fine, Sarah. Jerry helped me."

Jerry and the officer gently lay Kayla on a stretcher. Another EMT begins a saline drip solution and gives her a tetanus shot.

"Is Nicky...alive?" Kayla asks.

"Yes, thanks to Jerry," Sarah holds the door of the ambulance. "He faced off the monster before it could eat Nick."

"Monster?" the officer asks confused.

"Yes, a bear-panther thing. It's huge with big sharp fangs and claws that kill with one swipe." Sarah mimes with a swing of her arm, hand out like a claw.

"Sounds like the panther that escaped the Rockwell area about a year ago." The officer glances about placing his hand on his holster.

"Farmer...Blaine   was...was...feeding   it,"   Jerry   holds Kayla's hand.

"Really? Hmmm, Mr. Springer?" Jerry nods.

"Where is he?"

"He...died. Grim...malkin...took him."

"Grimalkin?"

"The monster!" Sarah slaps her thigh.

"It killed him?"

"I...don't...think so. He...didn't...have any...claw...claw marks...on him."

"We gotta find it. Hundreds of hunters were all over the state last time. Things are finally calming down— don't want that situation to happen again."

"Farmer...Blaine says...she's the last...one...of her...kind."

"Last one we know of, anyway."

Nick safely in the ambulance, the EMTs prepare Kayla to go into the vehicle next to him. "Jerry!" Kayla squeezes his hand. "I promise...we will go to the beach another day," she smiles weakly.

Jerry nods. He doesn't know what to say. "Thank you." Kayla's eyes droop. She blinks in an attempt to stay awake. "Thank you for making me feel like I'm not alone. We can survive horrible lives and go on to live good ones. Always remember, you're a good guy, Jerry."

Tears well in Jerry's eyes.

"And you're not stupid," Kayla continues. "I'll be alright. I hope to see you again...soon."

Jerry smiles. "I...want to...see you too." Kayla pulls his hand to her lips and kisses the back of it, surprising him. It makes him warm all over. She releases him and passes out. Jerry glances at the EMTs in alarm.

"She'll be okay. You can see her at the hospital.

Please step aside." Jerry moves. The EMTs slide Kayla into the ambulance and close the doors. "Good job on the tourniquet. It saved that guy's life."

Jerry blushes and smiles wide.

The police officer approaches Jerry. "Animal control and back-up is on the way to find Mr. Springer. Don't go anywhere."

Sarah gets into the back of the police car. The officer starts the engine and turns on the siren leading the ambulance down the lane. The other police car remains on the property. Jerry walks to his shack and puts on fresh clothing. He goes to the chicken coop to check on the chickens and secure the door. He thinks about everything that has happened and remembers the connection Farmer Blaine had with Grimalkin, the way she looked at him. Jerry felt a kinship with her too when the creature gazed into his very soul with her ochre eyes. *She has feelings. She understands me. She's been abused, and her mother was a killer too.*

Jerry decides to find her before they do. The officer is reading something in his car. Jerry slips across the yard toward the woods and follows spots of blood on a path to a huge old live-oak tree with an opening at its base. It appears to be hollow. He peers inside. A pair of yellow eyes glow at him. He jumps back and listens.

It is quiet.

Heart racing, he takes a deep breath and looks again. When his eyes adjust to the dark, he sees Grimalkin curled around Farmer Blaine—the stench so bad he holds his breath. There are bones of something that must have been huge scattered about the floor of the hollow tree; one of the bones is thick as his wrist. They are the remains of The Beast of Bladenboro.

Grimalkin lies gazing at him. She doesn't move. Blood from one of her front legs has pooled around her paw. There are scars scattered about her shoulder and neck where pellets from a shotgun got her. Even though none of these are fatal injuries, her breathing is rapid and shallow.

Jerry, his racing heart slows as fear turns to sympathy, crawls into the space. Grimalkin growls at first, until Jerry reaches out and touches her muzzle. His scent, similar to Farmer Blaine when he was alive, calms her. He strokes her head. She purrs and nuzzles into Farmer Blaine. The purring stops. Air escapes her chest never to return. Her breathing has ceased. Her ochre eyes fade. Jerry strokes her rough fur, no longer sensing her untamed spirit. Tears in his eyes, Jerry crawls out of the tree and sits. After several hours, the sun sets. He returns to his shack. The police car is gone.

*

Early the next morning, while Jerry sits in his shack eating a breakfast he made for himself, several vehicles roll up the lane into the drive. There are police cars, trucks, vans, and an ambulance. Men pile out holding guns. Two of them have bloodhounds. A cage is unloaded from one van.

The men split up—some going into the fields, others march into the woods. Jerry washes his dishes and gets a paper bag out of a drawer. He places cash he earned from working on the farm in it. He picks up the flip-phone Farmer Blaine gave him and the photo of his parents at the beach from the table and puts them into his bag. It's a hot and muggy August day.

He tucks his bag under one arm and begins walking un-noticed down the lane—golden oats blowing in the breeze on one side, tobacco with huge bright green leaves on the other.

"I'm...going...to the...beach."

Chapter 33

The Ocean

Jerry is determined to see the ocean. Kayla promised she would see him again. He is sure she won't. How could she? Her home is a hundred miles away and he can't stay at the farm. If Kayla is true to her promise, she will find him there. That's why he is walking directly east along a curvy road taking him through small towns. Folks see him walking with his full paper bag tucked under one arm. They offer him food, money, and rides as he walks along. He's lost count of how many times he's told, "Bless your heart". Folks like to talk, and Jerry is a good listener.

One man offers Jerry a job at his fruit stand in Topsail.

He takes the offer with no hesitation...but first, he must see the ocean. After five long days he walks over a ridge onto a boardwalk. At the end of it, before Jerry, is the ocean spreading far as he can see.

He's overwhelmed by the sight. The waves cresting and pounding against the shore soothe and terrify him at the same time. The warm sand tickles his feet. The salty mist is cool on his skin. It is more than what he imagined. Jerry sits at the edge of the surf feeling the cool water lick at his heels. He watches strange little beetle-like creatures dig in the wet sand every time the wash of a wave passes over them. He takes the framed picture of his parents out of the paper bag and gazes at the ochre photo. They're happy and smiling at the camera. Waves lick at their heels, like they do him now. He feels a cosmic connection to them.

He's warm and content in the moment until a little girl asks him if he would like to help her find shark's teeth.

"Shark's...teeth are...are in...a shark's...mouth.

You don't...want to...see that...do you?"

The little girl laughs. "You're funny. They look like this." She opens her hand to show him a black, small, pointed tooth.

"I thought...shark's...shark's teeth...are white?" *Is this little girl teasing me?*

"They turn black when they fall out." She tilts her head and smiles.

"Oh." Jerry realizes she's asking him to find teeth that have fallen out. "Now...that...makes sense." He learns yet another thing in the wide-open world.

He can't find a shark's tooth, but he enjoys the company. The many shapes and sizes of the shells amaze him. What lived in them and where are they now? The little girl doesn't know either.

The next day, after Jerry slept on the beach, he eats half of a burger he had saved. He rises to his feet, picks up his paper bag of valuables, brushes the sand from his pants, and begins to walk to the fruit stand where he will begin a new life. He spies a familiar shape in the distance. *It can't be her. I must be seeing things*--but as the shape nears, she begins waving her arms wildly. "Kayla!" Jerry breaks into a run. His heart thumps with each step. Kayla's lustrous long brown hair bounces, and her smile practically covers her face; eyes, wide and shining while she runs, Kayla reminds Jerry of one of those runners bringing the torch to light the Olympic cauldron and he's already lit.

They stop, mere feet away from each other...panting.

"This...is...the beach." He waves toward the waves.

Kayla laughs, "Yes, it is."

Jerry's happiness is complete. He has the beach and Kayla right here...and a whole new life waiting for him. She leans in and kisses him on the lips. The back of his throat tickles. The world is spinning. He might faint. It's the best feeling ever.

"How...did you...find me?" Jerry's smile is making his face ache.

"Uncle Mike brought me. I just needed a few stitches and a shot, and they sent me home." Kayla takes his hand while walk the boardwalk off of the beach. "I couldn't wait to look for you. I was afraid I would never see you again. We checked like four places. I told Uncle Mike that you would go directly east, so...here I am! Isn't it amazing?" She flings her arms around Jerry's neck. It's the happiest second day of his life.

Uncle Mike is waiting for them in his car. Kayla pulls Jerry into the back seat with her. Mike leans over the seat. "There you are. That was like finding a shark's tooth in a pile of shells. I am amazed."

"Me too. I...couldn't...find a...shark's tooth."

Uncle Mike laughs. "You're here now. Where to?"

"I...got a job..."

"Jerry got a job at a fruit stand. We'll have lunch and then take him there before we go home." Kayla grabs Jerry's hand. "Oh Jerry, I'm so glad we found you."

"Me...too." Jerry's glad he's sitting down. The dizziness isn't going away. Kayla kisses him on his hot cheek.

*

Before Kayla returns home, she gives Jerry a charging cord for his flip phone. She shows him how to charge it and promises him she will stay in touch. The owner of the fruit stand, Pete Willard, immediately takes Jerry under his wing. Like his old boss, Farmer Blaine Springer, Mr. Willard has a lot of things to teach him.

Jerry works hard. Mr. Willard even finds a place for

Jerry to live. His son, Keith needed a roommate...or "someone to keep an eye on him," as Mr. Willard tells Jerry in confidence.

Keith is a great roommate. He's why Jerry can talk better. Keith tells him, "Slow your brain down, man. Think, take a breath, and then talk." It works.

Jerry has a job and a good life now, but all he can think about is Kayla. Kayla, Kayla, Kayla. She calls him at least twice a week...sometimes more. He stops everything to listen to her gab about her day to him. Her voice makes him dizzy like the day she kissed him on the beach. He misses her, but he knows he will see her again someday.

Jerry wishes he could thank farmer Blaine Springer for giving him the start to his new life, and Grimalkin—things could have been different for her. She was used and hunted, confused and angry at the loss of the one human who understood and cared for her. Jerry saw pain in her eyes. He understood that pain--the ache of captivity and loss. He was given a second chance at life.

She wasn't.

The End

Chapter 34

Endnotes

This fictional story is based on the legend of the Beast of Bladenboro. Bladenboro, North Carolina has a yearly festival in October in remembrance of an event where several farm animals and pets where killed in 1954. Many swore it was the work of a huge black panther like creature. Hunters came from all over the country to shoot it, creating a fear someone would get seriously injured or killed. So, the mayor put a stop to it by claiming it was the work of a Bobcat. The panther in my story is a progeny of the creature.

In my research, North Carolina was home to panthers until the encroachment of civilization. A panther (or puma) hasn't been officially spotted in NC since 2011. A black panther is a melanistic (black pigmentation) big cat. It could be a Panther, Jaguar, Puma, Leopard, or Cougar. Though they may no longer naturally live here, North Carolina is home to 5 big cat farms and 11 zoos, most house pumas, tigers, and black panthers. The state is only 1 of 4 in the country who doesn't regulate the keeping of big cats. I had interviewed several people who claimed to have seen panthers. I believe it is totally feasible for a panther to escape one of these facilities.

I also want to recognize Tiger World in Rockwell, who run entirely on donations.

I belong to the Eastern Puma Research group and was a middle school teacher for 25 years, and a summer recreation director for 15.